Nightingale's Song

Also by Kate Pennington

Tread Softly
Brief Candle
Charley Feather

Nightingale's Song

Kate Pennington

Hodder
Children's
Books

a division of Hachette Children's Books

A Catalogue record for this book is available from the British Library

ISBN-10: 0 340 87875 4
ISBN-13: 9780340878750

Typeset in AGaramond by Avon DataSet Ltd,
Bidford-on-Avon, Warwickshire

Printed and bound in Great Britain by
Bookmarque Ltd, Croydon, Surrey

The paper and board used in this paperback by Hodder Children's Books
are natural recyclable products made from wood grown in
sustainable forests. The manufacturing processes conform to the
environmental regulations of the country of origin.

Hodder Children's Books
A division of Hachette Children's Books
338 Euston Road
London NW1 3BH

'Here lies William Cole, who was drowned on the 20th of March 1756 aged 19 years'

The new headstone darkened in the rain. The raw earth was sodden. A great storm lashed the graveyard. Out on the German Sea, boats were tossed on the crests of great grey waves. Wind tore at their rigging.

The earth of William Cole's freshly dug grave ran with water. Mud slid down the steep hillside towards the edge of the cliff where Charles Howard, riding officer of His Majesty's Excise Office, sat on horseback, staring out to sea. The night was black. He saw no sign, and knew there would be none until the storm abated.

The rain did not let up. It lashed the gravestones in the bleak churchyard and swept against the ruined walls of the abbey close by. William's grave gurgled; the wet earth shifted to expose the coffin lid. Was it the wind groaning through the gaping arches, or the disturbed soul of the drowned man?

Howard turned up the collar of his greatcoat and cursed the storm. He watched for a single shaft of light to pierce the gloom – a signal to the *Eagle* from the smugglers on shore. His horse shifted uneasily. He reined her in and kept his watch.

Behind him, the open grave yawned wide.

Part One

One

Though I had little heart for it that night as the storm raged, I stood beside the hearth and sang.

> *'We cast our nets in Skinningrove Wyke*
> *And fishes we caught nine,*
> *We had three to fry and three to dry*
> *And three . . .'*

'Tell the girl to stop that noise!' Thomas Hague snarled at my father, who was landlord at the Anchor Inn on Saltersgate.

'Maggie!' My father dismissed me from my place by the fire and so I gave up singing willingly enough.

'What's the matter, Tom? You're usually partial to a song from a pretty girl.'

This was my pa speaking, above the babble of voices in the inn and the wild roar of the storm outside. The wind blew smoke down the chimney stack and filled the room.

'There's a time for singing, which is not now, when boats in the harbour are likely to be dashed against the jetty and the *Eagle* waits offshore for the storm to blow itself out.' Hague leaned forward to rattle his pipe against the chimney breast.

'I hear the *Mary Ann* is lost,' someone said through the thick blue smoke. His face was only half lit by the oil lamp on the wall. 'She leaves two widows and a grieving mother on Boulby Bank.'

'All three men went down with her,' another confirmed.

There was a break in the chatter. Rain spattered the windows, the wind rattled at the door.

'"We cast our nets",' I hummed, only to stop myself thinking of the three drowned souls. A storm at sea is like an angry beast which devours all in its path.

'Aye, sing on, little Maggie!' Zak Trattles said to me with a lopsided leer. 'It cheers a man to hear the voice of an angel rising above the storm's might.'

But Tom Hague glowered at me across the room, calling for more ale, which I poured from a stone jug.

'. . . Believe me, William Cole's ghost walks tonight,' he told Mally Truefit, taking her on his knee and snaking his arm around her slender waist. 'You may hear his bones rattle by St Mary's churchyard if you venture out into the storm.'

Mally was uneasy, though she made a show of

6

mocking him. 'Is this ghost truly that of young William?' she asked.

'Certainly,' he breathed in her ear. 'He bears about him a pistol and a knife as long as my arm from elbow to fingertip which he used to slit a militiaman's throat before the sea claimed him at last!'

'Why, Tom, how can you believe in such old wives' tales as ghosts walking abroad at night?' Mally struggled to free herself. 'I took you for a bold man of the sea!'

'This is no tale,' he went on in a low, earnest voice that made the hairs on my neck stand on end. 'As true as I stand here, there is a skeleton risen from the grave in that churchyard on the east cliff! The flesh is already rotted from the bones. William walks down the steps towards the town!'

Mally shuddered. My father drew her roughly away from Hague and sent her to join me behind the bar. 'You see you frighten the wits out of her,' he told the smuggler. 'And she only widowed a month since.'

Hague laughed. 'George, I see you show a kindly interest in Mally!' he scoffed. 'And who can blame you for taking pity on a lonely widow?'

I glanced from my father to Mally, who straightened her bodice so that it came down low at the front. She pinned up some stray locks of fair hair, blushing as she did so.

'Do you believe William's ghost walks tonight?'

I asked her earnestly. I pictured the dead smuggler approaching down the abbey steps, through the narrow streets, his white bones rattling. He would come upon me as I slept and waken me with his terrible grin.

Mally shook her head. 'Don't listen to Hague's stories, Maggie,' she whispered back. 'He has his own reasons for frightening us, believe me!'

Nearby, Zak Trattles agreed with Mally. 'His mind is on the *Eagle* and her cargo,' he predicted, blinking his one good eye while the other socket gaped. 'Not on bones buried in the churchyard!'

'Hold your tongue!' Mally warned as Hague glanced our way. He noted the tall figure of James Peacock standing in the low entrance. The exciseman had come in from the storm, shaking off his greatcoat, which soon began to steam from the warmth of the fire.

Hague's mood darkened. 'What brings you from keeping respectable company at the Angel?' he demanded.

'Into this den of thieves, you mean?' Mr Peacock replied, taking off his hat and hanging it on a hook behind the door as if Tom Hague meant nothing in the world to him.

He went and sat at the opposite side of the fire to Hague and a smirking, sly man named Ned Bonnet, who was always in Hague's company, following him like a shadow, unless he was chasing the little flither pickers with their raised hems and blue petticoats, who are no older than I, and I am but thirteen years of age.

Flither pickers are the girls who walk out on to the rocks when the tide is low. They gather limpets to bait the fishermen's lines, and I would not do their hard labour for twice the meagre money they are paid. I had rather work for my supper alongside my father, bringing ale from the cellar and singing on occasion to soothe the fishermen who have been far out to sea and who face danger nightly to bring in their catch.

They do say I sing sweetly, and this I have from my mother, who caught a fever and died when I was two years old, and so I have no memory of her.

Ned took up his tune from Hague, sneering at Mr Peacock's efforts to warm his hands by the fire. 'Is it the ghost of William Cole that makes you shake and shudder so?' he mocked.

'I bested the thieving scoundrel when he was alive.' The exciseman grunted his reply, recalling for his audience that he had sent Cole to the assizes in York the year before he died. There the magistrate had pressed Cole into the King's navy for concealing two great ankers of French brandy in his mother's house at Town End. 'Fear not – his spirit will not trouble me from beyond the grave!'

Everyone looked to Hague to judge his response, but the villain ignored the jibe. 'Where's the girl?' he called to my father, busy bolting the door against the wind. 'My humour has changed for the better. Tell her she must stand by me and sing a cheerful song.'

At this my heart thumped and I attempted to hide my slight frame behind Mally and her wide, rustling skirts, for I did not care to get too close to the most notorious smuggler on the north-east coast of England. Hague would as soon stick a scaning knife in a man's back as give him the time of day. Besides, he has a sharp look about his features, enough to cut you with a glance, with his long, thin nose and mean slit of a mouth. His forehead bears a scar from temple to brow.

But my father called me. 'Child, you will sing for your supper after all!'

There was no escape, so, with Cole's ghost rattling at the door behind me to come in, and with Hague and Ned Bonnet to greet me ahead, I stepped out to sing.

My song was of lovers whose families stood in their way. He was low-born, she the daughter of a wealthy man, and so they met and wooed in secret. I sang the words in a pure voice, telling how the maid swore to forsake her rich life and elope with the penniless whaling man who sailed the frozen northern seas.

Behind me the fire crackled. Hague listened contentedly, tapping his toe to the tune.

However, the tale ends badly. The maid catches a fever and falls ill, and when the time comes for the lovers to elope she lies on her deathbed and he must stand below the window calling her name in vain, which his poor ghost does to this day.

'Enough!' Hague growled as I came to a doleful end. 'Do you call this a song to cheer a man on a stormy night?'

''Tis a song of love,' I replied, for though I am afraid of Hague, I have a quick tongue and a ready answer for all. 'A love song warms the heart, for sure.'

'If a man has a heart to warm,' Zak muttered, loud enough for folk to hear.

Mr Peacock, still sitting by the hearth, praised my voice. 'Maggie lives up to the family name,' he told my father. 'She sings sweeter than any nightingale.'

'Aye and George keeps her closer than any caged bird,' Ned Bonnet leered, looking for a glimpse of my ankles, as if I were any ordinary flither girl.

I stared back at his broad, rough face spoiled by angry red boils. My gaze was even and defiant.

At this moment there was a heavy knock on the door and a rattling of the latch.

Behind the bar, her head still full of ghostly tales, Mally jumped in fright. She turned to my father.

'Open the door,' he said calmly.

So she hurried across to slide the bolt, and in strode a stocky man by the name of Charles Howard, a riding officer for Mr Peacock, whose job it is to patrol the cliffs, looking out for signals from the ships that hover offshore. The wind and rain followed him into the room.

Howard took in the company, noting Hague and Ned gathered hugger-mugger by one side of the fire and Mr Peacock to the other. 'No signal as yet,' he told the latter in a loud voice, meanwhile keeping a beady eye on the smugglers. 'The storm tide rides high against the rocks. And my horse suffers from the wind and rain.'

'We will give her food and shelter at the Angel,' Peacock replied, striding across the room for his hat and coat. 'I will walk there with you.'

I wondered that they let Hague know their plan, for now it was clear that there was no watch kept along the east cliff and the *Eagle* might land her smuggled goods unhindered. Then again, perhaps it was a trick which the excisemen played.

Charles Howard took a mug of ale from Mally and supped it down before they left. 'I rode by the open grave of William Cole,' he reported with a knowing look at Zak and Mally. 'The rain has washed away the earth, thanks to the poor work of the gravediggers.'

'Hah!' Hague's cold laughter rose above the gasps. 'What did I say? Will Cole comes for you, sir, from beyond the grave!'

And though none wanted to believe him, all imagined the pale white figure of the ghost on the dark hillside, making its way to its old haunts – to the inns and quaysides, through the crooked streets and tumbledown yards, past the smokehouses and pigsties and down the dark alleyways in search of those who had wronged him.

It was late and all had left the inn, save Mally, Zak Trattles, Hague and Ned Bonnet. I longed for my bed, but I knew there was still much to do.

'The tide has turned and is taking the storm with it,' my father told Hague with a knowing wink. 'We will have a peaceful night after all.'

Hague had drunk his fill of ale and was in no hurry to leave.

Bonnet, though, was eager for action. 'It is time to give the signal,' he insisted. 'I will light the lamp and bring Hart and Penny to wait in Gin Yard.'

'Not yet,' Hague insisted. 'We will delay an hour and keep the excisemen out of their beds!'

In the battle of wits between Mr Peacock and the smugglers, Hague liked to amuse himself.

As Mally had said, on a night such as this he would spread stories of ghosts and foul spirits abroad to keep simple folk in their houses and leave the streets empty for him to go about his business.

Then he would likely as not mislead the excisemen over the time he would row his boat out to the ship where he would take on board kegs of brandy and gin from France, parcels of tobacco from the New World and counterfeit coins made in Holland.

Still under cover of darkness, the men would row back with their cargo to land in any one of a hundred narrow coves hidden from the excisemen's view. From there they would send their goods before dawn on pack-horses across the wide moor that rose above the town, bringing a quantity of spirits, tobacco and perhaps tea back home with them to store in the cellars and tunnels that wove like a honeycomb under the streets and houses.

'Cat and mouse!' Hague would say of himself and Peacock. 'And His Majesty's cat will never catch this mouse, though he spends his whole life in the attempt!'

My father yawned now and made signs that he was on the side of Ned Bonnet and was ready to act. 'The captain of the *Eagle* will grow uneasy if he waits longer. Let Ned send the signal now.'

The flickering fire had cast Hague's features into shadow, but I could see that he was the only one amongst us who remained alert and listening, as if it were midday.

He noted Zak and Mally lingering at the bar and straight away told my father to send them out. 'We will wait until midnight,' he declared as the door closed on them. 'Then we will act.'

Two

It was my role on these nights to open the secret door from the ale cellar into the concealed tunnel that went from the inn under Saltersgate and ended in a dark storeroom inhabited only by rats and spiders. I would stand ready with oil lamp in hand and key to the secret door hanging from my waist, waiting for the sounds of a single pack-horse wending its way in darkness down Saltersgate and stopping at our door.

Then all would be flurry and bluster as the parcels of tobacco and kegs of spirits landed with mighty thumps on the cobbles. My father, standing guard, would unlock the main door and Hague and Ned would burst in, staggering under the weight of the smuggled cargo. Down into the cellar it would come and I would turn the lock and thrust open the door on its rusty hinges, leading the way with my lamp to the damp, pitch-black storeroom beyond.

By no means did I like this work. Indeed my heart would almost jump clear of my ribs for fright, what with the excisemen lurking nearby and always the chance that we would be caught. And the ghosts troubled me, though my head said there was no truth in them. Besides that, the rats in the cellar scuttled under my skirt, between my feet, their sharp claws rattling against the stone flags. They entered my sleep and ran through my dreams for many nights after.

Tonight, however, Hague seemed in a mood to be perverse. He talked long with my father, always glancing in my direction, my father shaking his head at first, then seemingly giving way to Hague, as all men must.

Hague has within these three years bludgeoned two townsmen to death with an oar sawn off at the end for this purpose. There are no soldiers in town to defend us, and so we must fear for our lives if we cross Hague and refuse to do his will.

'Maggie, you will go out this night with Ned and help set the signal to the captain on board ship.' My father spoke reluctantly. He is a plain man who cares for me in his way, and would not have me put in danger.

I frowned and drew back into the shadows. I could see Hague watching me through narrowed eyes and Ned's horrid, slack-jawed grin.

'Put your shawl about your shoulders,' my father insisted gently, coming to me and handing me the garment. 'No harm will come. The business will be carried out as usual.'

'I had rather stay here,' I protested weakly. Then I

made an excuse. 'I fear William Cole's ghost will seize me and drag me into the world beyond.'

Hague laughed. 'Ned here will protect you. I fancy he likes you, Maggie!'

This made me shudder and shrink further. Then it was Ned's turn to laugh and seize me by the arm, almost lifting me off my feet as he rushed me out into the dark night.

'Bring her with you to Gin Yard!' Hague instructed before the door closed.

As soon as I could I wrenched myself free from Ned and ran ahead. 'I will come with you to light the lamp,' I declared. 'But you must not lay hands on me, or I will scratch and bite like a cat!'

'Oho!' he cried, blundering after me. 'Bold words. Yet I could seize you and snap you in two if I had the mind, Maggie. You are so thin, and not like a cat at all, but like a dark-eyed rabbit caught in a snare!'

'Do not touch me!' I warned, glad to turn the corner on to the bridge across the river, then into the shipbuilding yard on Bagdale Beck, where we were to set light to the spout lantern which would shine clear out to sea.

This done, we received a short, clear signal directly back from the captain of the *Eagle*, and all was ready for Hague and his men to row out to the ship.

'Come!' Ned ordered, taking me once more by the arm.

We hurried back across the bridge to meet Hague and his accomplices in Gin Yard, overlooking the harbour. Hague stood with a lantern, his collar pulled up around his sharp face, his eyes flicking restlessly here and there.

'Ah!' he said, spying me and dragging me forward to show off to Solomon Hart and Jim Penny, who were as vicious a pair of rogues as the town of Whitby could boast. 'Here is little Maggie Nightingale come to entertain us with her songs as we row out to sea!'

The news sent a fresh arrow of fear through my body. 'I will not!' I declared. 'I will not set foot from this shore!'

No more said than Hague lifted me clean off my feet and dashed me down in the boat by his side. The three other men climbed in after us.

'I am not sure of George Nightingale,' Hague explained as the three seized their oars and began to row. 'I have a suspicion that he means to inform against me one day, yet with his daughter in the boat with us, it will not happen this night at least.'

At this I stifled a startled cry and gripped the side of the boat. Though it rocked and there was only darkness ahead, I knew I must stay quiet, for there was no escape. I sat and silently cursed Tom Hague for his cruelty to me and my father, dreading the waves that were to come.

Three

Thick clouds hid the stars above. The strong tow of the tide speeded our way across the waves towards the *Eagle*, which we could not see though we knew she was there.

'Give us a sign, damn you!' Ned Bonnet cursed, pulling at his oars with all his might.

Water slapped against the sides of our shallow-bottomed boat, spraying up into our anxious faces.

'How will we find the ship without a light to guide our way?' Jim Penny complained, almost ready to turn about and head for shore.

Hague sat beside me, looking and listening. He glanced over his shoulder at the bulk of the cliffs behind, judging that the men must pull twenty strokes to the right and then keep in a straight line with the outline of the abbey. 'It will bring us to the ship soon enough,' he insisted.

Sure enough, a black shape loomed ahead – the hull of a great two-masted sloop rolling in the waves, waiting for the arrival of our tiny coble. Hague stood up, cupping his hands around his mouth to yell to the men on board the sloop. 'Captain Rijks, we are ready to receive your cargo! Lower away!'

And now we drew close enough to see men on deck, busily lowering ropes over the side, and at the ends of these ropes hung the kegs of spirits and parcels of tobacco wrapped in sailcloth. They swung over our heads, waiting to be untied by Hart and Penny, with Ned and Hague keeping the boat steady as they worked and myself sitting in stark terror at what they were about. Three seven-gallon kegs were safely stowed. A fourth was on its way when there was a flash of bright red light from the cliff and the sound of thunder cracking.

'Cannon fire!' Hague cried, before the shot landed in the sea with a mighty splash not thirty paces from us.

Another flash followed, and again the mighty bang. Hart and Penny ducked low in the boat, while Hague and Ned made haste with the final keg of spirits. This time, the aim was better than before. The cannonball sped from the cliff top towards the *Eagle* and landed not ten yards from us.

'Damn those militiamen!' Ned spat and snarled more curses towards land as our small boat rocked and all but capsized.

I crouched low in the prow of the boat, sick with terror, my clothes wringing wet from the seawater that washed over us.

A third and then a fourth cannon was fired, lighting up the cliff so that the ruins of the abbey glowed behind.

The captain of the *Eagle* leaned over the rail and bade us make haste away. 'Take what you have and make good your escape,' he yelled to Hague. 'If I take a shot in the side and the ship is holed, we're dead men!'

So Ned cut the last rope and let the keg tumble into the boat. It rocked so hard that I thought we should capsize, and so I prayed for my soul and called out my father's name in desperation.

Hague thrust me aside and called up once more. 'Never fear, Captain Rijks, I will throttle the man who betrayed us to the militia and brought this cannon fire raining down on our dishonest heads!'

I struggled up from the floor of the boat. 'It was not my father!' I cried. 'You must not harm him!'

Hague struck at me with his strong forearm and I fell against a wooden keg. He ordered the oarsmen to haste away from the tall ship, which set its sails and began to pull away, out of reach of the cannons. Meanwhile, we hurried off into the darkness, making for the secret coves where the militia could not discover us.

'Too close for comfort,' Hague muttered, gazing up at the last of the cannon fire.

I sobbed in the darkness, my mind battered by

dreadful thoughts, my eye on Hague's long knife carried in a leather scabbard fixed at his side. The men rowed hard.

Sick of my crying, Hague reached down and put a hand over my mouth. 'Your father is safe,' he muttered. 'I would bet my life on the name of the traitor, and George is not his first, nor Nightingale his last!'

'Who then?' Ned heard the bottom of the boat scrape on to pebbles and quickly leaped out with Hart and Penny to drag us on to the shore. Overhead, black rocks loomed.

'Zak Trattles is our man,' Hague replied as he thrust me out of the boat before him. 'The turncoat lurks in corners and runs with his tales to Peacock, and by God I'll gouge out the villain's good eye and leave him blind as a mole to grope his way about this earth for what he has done!'

The threat was delayed, however, for there was more urgent business to hand. First the men must unload the kegs and roll them up the narrow beach. This done, Hague gave a whistle which brought a man and his pack-horse down a steep track. The man lay in wait, ready to load the horse's panniers then set off across the moor top to Hobhole, where there was a rough thatched cottage which served as a secret hiding-place for the smuggled goods. All was to be achieved under cover of darkness.

The business was done without words. A keg was

loaded to either side of the horse and the man turned and led the horse back up the track. Hague then ordered Penny and Hart to heave one keg apiece on to their shoulders and the group of us followed the courier. We soon reached the cliff top and turned towards the town.

'Peacock will have his eyes peeled for us,' Hague warned as we approached the first houses. 'There will be soldiers everywhere.'

Very well, I thought. *This night I have survived being kidnapped by a notorious smuggler and being fired upon by cannons. What is a mere soldier with a musket to me?* And so I grew bold, though I shivered after my soaking at sea. After all, I knew the yards and alleyways of the town as well as any other, and better than any militiaman.

Hart and Penny stooped under the weight of the kegs. We crept along in secret, so that by the time we reached the top of Saltersgate, their legs buckled. Then Hague and Ned shouldered the burdens and sent the two men scuttling off. That left me to lead the way to the Anchor, glancing sideways into silent passages, listening for footsteps, fearing that the night was too quiet and thick for comfort, with all doors barred and every house still as death.

'Make haste!' Hague hissed as I hesitated by Luke Crispin the barber's door, just three from my own house.

I peered down the crooked, worn steps that led to the harbour side, suspecting a noise – maybe nothing more than a cat or a rat. The pause made Ned run into Hague from behind, and the two men stumbled sideways against the barber shop door.

Then suddenly the night erupted once more – this time with red-coated men bearing rifles, running up from the wharf, and others charging from the head of Saltersgate, so that we three were soon trapped.

Hague swore and dropped his barrel, rolling it savagely towards the men who approached up the steps. It crashed into them, splitting open as it bounced against a wall. Gin ran into the gutter, under the feet of the sprawling soldiers. Quick as lightning, townsmen appeared out of nowhere, carrying jugs which they used to scoop up the precious liquid.

And still armed men ran at us down the main street, raising their rifles and firing. There was a cry as Ned was hit and went down.

Hague seized the next barrel and sent it spinning into the path of the second group, giving him time to grab my arm and run for cover. Meanwhile more doors flew open and our neighbours ran out, pitching into the struggle and doing their utmost to prevent the soldiers from making progress.

Everywhere there was confusion. More shots were fired. My father flung open our door and stood in the street, his strong frame between me and the approaching soldiers. Hague and I ran for the inn, slipping in with only a second to spare.

'The tunnel!' my father muttered to us. 'You have the key?'

I nodded.

'Then go!' he urged, turning to bar the way of the first soldier who approached.

I heard a scuffle, a shot and a loud gasp, followed by a groan.

'Go forward!' Hague ordered as I attempted to turn back. He drove me behind the bar and down the cellar steps.

I struggled, but when he drew the knife from his belt and held it to my throat I was forced to do as he said, until we reached the concealed entrance to the tunnel.

'The key!' Hague rasped, turning to see if we were pursued.

I grasped for the key at my waist while Hague dragged aside the barrels which hid the entrance. Then I loosened the key and thrust it into the villain's hands, thinking that my job was done.

'Stay!' he warned, turning the key in the lock.

I felt my wrist seized once more. 'Let me go to my father!' I begged.

But no, he would drag me on and lock the door after us, thrusting me onwards. We went like blind men, feeling our way in utter darkness. And now there were no sounds from above, only the swish of my skirt against the damp, mouldy wall, until we came to the chamber I have mentioned.

Here I sank to the cold floor, my mind in a whirl, my body trembling. All around, fat rats scrambled and ran until Hague took out his tinderbox and struck a light. Then they froze in the sudden flare, their beady eyes glittering.

'Please let me go!' I sobbed, for I was at the end of my courage.

'No, Maggie, I will keep you by my side, for I may have need of you,' Hague replied grimly. He used the glaring light to find a rough stool upon which he sat.

I stared in dismay at his face – at the deep sockets of his eyes and dark, overhanging brow, the long nose and crooked slit of a mouth. It was a face that would not relent, and so I held back my pleas.

We waited in that dreadful underground place for what seemed like many hours, not knowing what had taken place above our heads. No one came searching for us beyond the locked door of the tunnel and we heard no noise.

At last Hague decided it was safe to emerge. In the blackest of moods, he ordered me to walk ahead of him until we came to the door. He turned the key quietly in the lock.

Here was the ale cellar, as before, except that one or two barrels lay on their sides. Here were the stone steps up to ground level, with here a soldier's button torn off in haste and now lying on the ground and there a raw mark on the stone wall where sharp metal had scraped against it.

'Hah, a fight!' Hague commented.

My heart beat rapidly as we came up into the inn. The room was empty, the pewter jugs gleaming dully on a shelf above the hearth. 'Father?' I called softly.

Hague bade me be silent, stepping quickly to the door, which he opened a crack to let in the daylight.

We had spent the whole night trapped like the rats in that deep dungeon. Now I blinked in the light, looking in vain for the tall, strong figure of my father who would tell me we were safe, that the soldiers had gone away and all was well. Instead, it was Mally Truefit who pushed at the door.

Hague frowned uneasily then let her in. 'What news?' he demanded.

'Oh!' she cried, her fair hair hanging about her shoulders, her eyes red from weeping. ''Tis bad!' she moaned, making as if to throw her arms around me.

Hague stepped in between us. 'Tell me quickly!'

My wild gaze flew here and there – from Mally to the knife at Hague's side, to a stain on the stone doorstep, dark and wide and the colour of blood.

'Poor little Maggie!' Mally groaned, pushing past Hague and taking me by both wrists and holding me at arm's length. She gazed deep into my eyes.

'Tell me,' I murmured, my breath almost gone from me, my heart full of dread.

''Tis George, your father,' she whispered, her own voice broken with grief. And I was sure of what had happened before she said it, hearing once again the sound of gunshot and a mighty groan, the slump of a body across the threshold.

'He is dead,' she told me. 'Killed by the militia and his body laid out by the open door of St Mary's church.'

Four

I thought my world should end then and there.

My father dead and I an orphan.

His blood spilled for the world to see.

'He was a good man.' Mally tried to comfort me. 'He died defending you, Maggie, and when I came upon him in his dying breath and stooped low to hear, his last words were of you.'

I cried no tears. It felt as though the blood were drained from my own body and lay with *his* dear blood on the stone step.

'They shot and killed Ned too,' Mally told Hague. Then the townsmen fought the soldiers off and overpowered them as they tried to pursue you and the girl. At half past midnight Peacock ordered the retreat.'

'How many dead on their side?' Hague asked, cool as you like.

'One – stabbed by Ned as he lay dying. Ned cursed the man who tried to stop the blood pouring from his wound and swore that he would drag him into hell with him.'

'Ha!' Hague smiled grimly. He had heard enough and was anxious to leave. He pulled me out into the street.

'Wait. Where are you taking her?' Mally protested, pulling at me by the other arm.

'What is it to you?' Hague answered roughly, looking this way and that.

'I swore I would take care of the girl. 'Twas a sacred promise!'

'Which you will now be forced to break,' Hague sneered, snatching me away.

I kicked at his shin and bit his wrist, breaking into a frenzy and screaming that I would not go. But Hague soon overcame me, pulled out his knife and turned it on Mally.

She cowered against the wall, her face deathly white, her lips trembling.

Hague advanced and pressed the tip of the knife to her throat. 'It would be foolish to stand in my way, mistress. I say the girl comes with me!'

With this he thrust her away and marched with me down empty Saltersgate towards the harbour, taking me God knew where.

But we did not get far. As I have said, the yards and alleyways of this town are many and may conceal any number of enemies lying in wait. So as Hague and I came into Gin Yard, disturbing seagulls which pecked at scraps of meat thrown from a window high above, a group of redcoats sprang out from every direction, and with them were James Peacock and Charles Howard, there to see that the arrests were safely made.

In this fresh crisis, I did not sink to the ground in surrender but fought with hands and feet, my dark hair flying loose, my fists pummelling the chests of soldiers who flew at me. By my side, Hague slashed his long knife through the air, crying out in rage against Zak Trattles and others who might have betrayed him.

'Take care not to harm the girl!' Peacock cried.

I felt myself pinned to the wall and found that my hands were quickly tied with strong rope. Then I watched Hague weave his flashing blade, striking out without landing a blow. Five or six men opposed him, darting clear of the knife, and at last one came up from behind, pinning Hague's arms to his side and thrusting him down to the ground with his knee. Two other soldiers disarmed him and thrust the long barrels of their rifles between his shoulder blades so that he lay like a fish harpooned on the quay.

Then my heart leaped when I thought I should be free from this terrible man and my only thought was to flee up the steps to St Mary's where my poor father lay.

But the captain of the dragoons soon dashed these hopes.

'Take them both to the magistrate's house,' he ordered his redcoats. 'Get the good man out of his bed, for we must send these two villains to York and lodge them safely in the city gaol before sundown!'

I was plunged into despair at this and appealed to Mr Peacock, who had known me well. 'Sir,' I cried, 'you must tell him that I am no smuggler, and neither was my father!'

Peacock shook his head. 'I am sorry, child. I cannot swear this in front of a court,'

''Tis true! Hague forced us to provide storage for him, on pain of our lives!'

Still the exciseman shook his head. 'I cannot swear it before God. You were on the boat that rowed out to the *Eagle* last night, were you not?'

'Taken there by force!' I cried. 'Ask him. Let him tell you himself!'

Peacock turned to Hague, who had been raised from the ground and stood with his hands tied, a look of murder in his eyes. His hard mouth uttered no word.

'Take them,' the captain said again.

This time the soldiers seized us and marched us from the quay, and as we went, my last hope of seeing my dear father on this side of the grave drained with every step.

We were taken straight away to be examined by Mr Robert Bethell, an East Riding Justice of the Peace, who lived on the west bank of the River Esk. His new dwelling-house overlooked the rocky inlet known as

Abraham's Bosom, far from the smells of tar and sawdust in the shipbuilders' yards.

Mr Bethell was a small man who wore gold-rimmed glasses, and he peered over the top of them at the two villains brought before him that Friday morning in October, that is to say at myself and Hague, still with our hands tied and our clothes stained and torn. What he saw he did not seem to like,

'It has long been my wish to bring this violent man to justice,' he told Mr Peacock, pointing at Hague. 'These smugglers have very much in their power to distress us, and here is one of the hardest-featured men it has ever been my misfortune to encounter.'

At this Hague snorted and held his head high.

'I congratulate you both,' Mr Bethell told Peacock and the captain who stood next to him. 'It takes me by surprise, however, that Hague should have such a youthful accomplice.' Here he turned his attention to me and studied me closely. 'She is very small, and yet we know the powers of wickedness do enter young souls and take up their abode.'

'I am no smuggler!' I told the old man.

The captain broke in over me. 'The girl carries the key to a secret chamber under the Anchor Inn, sir. Without her, the smugglers could not run their unlawful trade.'

I expected no help from Hague on this occasion and so I kept my face turned from him.

'So young and pure in feature,' the justice sighed, staring into my face. Then he took written depositions from Peacock's hand and read them quickly before signing another piece of paper, which was the document committing us to trial at the session house in York as soon as proceedings could be brought against us there.

'You have sound witnesses?' Mr Bethell asked, peering over his glasses at Peacock.

'Sir, we have signed statements from Zak Trattles, bookmaker of Church Street, and from Luke Crispin, barber of Saltersgate, both men of good repute.'

I glanced at Hague and saw the flash of violence in his eyes at mention of these names.

Peacock went on. 'We know besides that though Hague has no settled way of living, yet that he lives like a gentleman, hunting with hounds and drinking with men of property whenever he may.'

'Enough,' the justice concluded, sealing the papers with wax and handing them to the captain. 'You may carry the prisoners by coach safely to York gaol. Make sure that none hinder you on the road.'

With this the good gentleman left us to attend to his breakfast.

I will not recount the journey across the moors, nor the anguish I suffered as I left the place of my birth. Only that I took one last look at the red-tiled roofs as we rose above them up the steep hill towards Sleights and felt certain that I should nevermore set eyes on the slanting doorways, leaning chimney pots, alleys and wharves. Nor would I see the ruined abbey high on the cliff, or visit the churchyard where my father's body would be laid.

May he rest more peacefully than many who are buried there, I said to myself, my heart wrenched, twisted and torn.

Beside me sat Hague, the man responsible for all my misfortunes, who looked neither right nor left during all the long journey, but who brooded silently, as if planning his revenge on those who had betrayed him.

Five

'Forty guineas was the price on my head!' Hague told a gaggle of fellow prisoners in the Castle Gaol at York.

We had arrived at dusk and entered the great stone prison house, to be met by roars and curses, and all manner of stench, clamour and nastiness. We were taken from the coach and promised by the captain that we should enjoy good lodgings here, for there was straw on the floor and raised wooden beds for us to sleep on, and so we must count our blessings.

I must confess I found it hard to do so, for the gaol in York seemed the gateway to hell.

'Zak Trattles sold me for forty guineas!' Hague boasted, strutting through the crowd of ragged beings who clamoured around him.

''Tis Thomas Hague!' one whispered, recognising the smuggler's lean features. 'He is brought down at last!'

Thomas Hague! The whisper flew round the gaol. *He has cheated the hangman these twenty years, but the three-legged mare claims even the likes of Hague!*

Hague kept me by his side. I felt hands try to grab me; faces seamed with dirt and sweat peered into mine through the gloom.

Because his name was known by scoundrels the length of the east coast, there was many an offer of beds and other comforts such as meat to eat and liquor to drink. Indeed, the gaoler himself soon approached Hague with a pitcher of fresh ale and bade him welcome.

'So, Mister Hague,' he said, with a courteous bow, 'you will soon have your date with the hangman, but you must make merry while you can. Invite any gentleman of your acquaintance to visit you here and rest assured they will be provided with the best ale and spirits, and any other hospitality I can offer.'

'Aye, for a price!' Hague grunted, snatching the ale from him and drinking it down. He seemed set on taking the gaoler's advice. 'Gather round,' he told the prisoners. 'Tell me, does any know of a friend or neighbour willing to ride to Whitby at dawn and seek out one-eyed Zak Trattles and Luke Crispin for me?'

'Aye!' came the cry. 'I have a cousin who will do the deed. Shall the turncoats be stabbed or shot?'

'Strangled,' Hague said, his eyes narrowed and glittering. 'Then thrown from the cliff into the German Sea!'

This cheered the crowd. Their spirits rose higher

when Hague offered six of the nearest prisoners a share of his pitcher.

I noted among them women as well as men, and girls not much more grown than I myself. All were wretches of the lowest degree, all ragged, some barefoot, many staring meanly at me and prodding me as if I were a goose at the Christmas Fair.

'How came you here?' a girl of my own age demanded. She had long, lank hair about her shoulders, a skin marred by smallpox and scarcely any teeth in her poor head.

'By coach,' I replied innocently.

At which she laughed and explained that she meant to say, what crime had I committed.

'None at all!' said I, keeping my skirts close about me and backing against the wall.

'Oh, "none at all"!' voices echoed, hooting and mocking. 'We're all innocent here, until the noose is around our necks. Then we readily confess our sins and so make a good end!'

My eyes rolled and I struggled for breath at the thought.

'Give her room!' Hague ordered, seeing me about to faint. 'Fear not, Maggie, they have yet to try us and, once I have dispensed with Trattles and Crispin, I will hire as good a set of witnesses as may be found!'

'All paid for in counterfeit coins!' a bystander laughed.

At any rate, the crowd dispersed a little and Hague sat me down on a wooden bed close by. 'You must harden yourself,' he told me in a low voice. 'You are not home at the Anchor now!'

I said I wished with all my heart that I was, or else dead with my dear father in St Mary's church. I sat with my head lowered and my hand over my mouth and nose to block out the stench.

Hague forgot me for a while, busily drinking and making acquaintance with the most notorious of our fellow prisoners – namely, a housebreaker named Ruth Hollings who had escaped the hangman because she was with child, John Page, convicted of more than three hundred robberies upon the King's highway, and a common pickpocket named Burly Jack, though I can't say his true name, for it was never used in my hearing.

'Maggie Nightingale!' Hague called at last. 'Come forward!'

Reluctantly I stood up to do as I was bid.

The toothless girl hung by my side, feeling at the stuff of my skirt, which was blue Irish linen, with a petticoat of white cambric. I wore a bodice of paler blue, and though all was stained by the sea, the clothes were of some value, compared with the rags all around.

'Now you may come into your own and show the ladies and gentlemen of the gutter your talents!'

I frowned and shook my head, not wanting to be mocked.

'Maggie sings like a bird!' Hague announced. 'Merely to hear her is to have your spirits raised as if you sat in a woodland glade on a fine summer's afternoon!'

'Sing!' people urged, until I had no choice and must stand in the middle of them and clear my throat. I closed my eyes and tilted back my head

'The trees they grow so high and the leaves they grow so
   green.
The day is past and gone, my love, that you and I have
   seen.'

At this the crowd fell silent, all staring at me and starting to think differently about me, as if my voice raised me above them.

'Ah, 'tis a pretty song,' someone murmured.

'But it ends sadly,' another said.

'It's a cold winter's night, my love, when I must bide alone,
For my bonny lad is young but a-growing.'

They say music soothes the savage breast, and it was true that there was quiet among the prisoners as my voice soared through that foul den. I opened my eyes to find that some wept and many hung their heads as if ashamed, my toothless shadow among them.

I finished the song, which ends in cold death, and even in this dreadful place brought on a mood of thoughtfulness among all who listened.

My new friend wept a little and so I sat with her on the nearest bed and asked her history.

'My name is Betty,' she confessed. 'My mother lies sick at home with three babies under five years and I have no father. I was taken for stealing a piece of brocade from a house on Gillygate and the constable brought me here, where I may rot for all anyone cares.'

It was my turn to hang my head. 'Will no one speak for you at your trial?' I asked.

Betty shook her head. 'The lady of the house will bear witness against me, though her husband was not so cruel. He said I looked wretched and was most likely driven to my crime by desperation. The wife would have none of it and swore she would see me hanged.'

So I saw that my own misery was shared by many within those walls, and that the drinking and singing was a poor disguise to cover their wretchedness.

The first night in the prison I slept little. Hague kept me at his side and I saw that the villain had a peaceful night, helped on by the ale he had drunk and the jokes he had shared with our fellow prisoners. He awoke demanding breakfast and sending to the gaoler for cured ham and eggs, washed down with good green tea.

I ate nothing and suffered much.

Before noon a chaplain came to visit me to make me confess my crimes. He was a round man with legs like the hams Hague had feasted on, a great belly and chins that descended on to his chest. He looked at me in sorrow.

'Tut,' he began, shaking his head. 'So young and pretty, yet so corrupt.'

I drew myself up to my full height and held my head high, for my father's sake.

'What is my sin?' I challenged.

'Tut!' he said again. 'Is your heart so hardened that you can look into the face of God the Father and deny your crime?'

'I speak the truth,' I said plainly. Out of the corner of my eye I could see Hague listening to our every word, waiting to pounce if I spoke against him. 'I have done nothing wrong.'

The chaplain pushed out his fleshy bottom lip, looking for all the world like a pouting child who could not get its way. 'It will go better for you if you confess,' he warned. 'Indeed, it is your only way to escape the hangman.'

'Let them hang me, then,' I replied, sounding more bold than I felt.

'If you confess they will send you as a convict to the New World, where you may start a new life.'

'Aye, as a slave,' Hague cut in. 'Do not listen to the

villain, Maggie. Confession or not, they will hang us anyway!'

This talk of hanging made me tremble, as ever. I turned away from the chaplain and lost myself amongst the horde of prisoners clamouring at the barred door for food and drink. When next I glanced around I saw the man of God sharing a platter of beef and fresh bread with Hague, washed down with a good Madeira wine.

'Maggie, you must be brave!' Mally told me. She had made the journey from Whitby and come to the prison with food she hoped would tempt me – gingerbread and other sweet delicacies – and with news from home.

The sight of her tall slim figure and fair hair had made me break out in a fit of weeping. I had been four days in prison, counting each minute, and each hour falling further into despair. 'They will hang me,' I cried, clinging to her and wishing for a miracle that would sweep me out of here, back on to the bracing cliffs and rocky shore.

'Hush!' she said. 'The judge may take pity on you. Be upright and look him in the eye. They say Justice Robert Carr may melt before a pair of bright brown eyes and a pretty face.'

Then Mally told me that our trial was set for the next assizes, which was in three days' time.

'Justice Carr, you say?' Hague broke away from conversation with two men who were his visitors. He came to join us. 'And what of the witnesses?' he asked Mally, seizing her by the arm and pressing her back against the wall.

'Trattles is dead,' she reported flatly. 'Choked by a rope from Bagdale boatyard and his body washed up in the harbour.'

Hague nodded and his eyes narrowed. 'And Crispin?'

'In hiding,' Mally told him reluctantly. 'They say Peacock has him in a safe house.'

At this Hague hurried back to his visitors and spoke earnestly with them.

Maggie took me further to one side. 'Your father is buried,' she told me gently, her grey eyes moist. 'The whole town came up to the churchyard to see him lowered into his grave.'

I wept freely and told her that my life was at an end. 'I have no father and no mother, Mally. I am bound to the side of one of the worst villains in the whole of Yorkshire, who has his reasons for wanting me to die next to him, though God knows what they may be!'

'People pray that Hague will see the end of the hangman's rope,' Mally confessed. 'Indeed, they hold their breath until it is accomplished. But for you, Maggie, their prayers are that justice will be done and that you will return to us.'

I longed to believe in the strength of those prayers, but then I looked around me at the poor beggars and thieves, the sea of hopeless souls. I felt sure that I would drown among them.

'I am bound to Hague,' I repeated dully. 'His fate is mine. If he hangs by the neck until he is dead, then so must I.'

Six

Hague and I came before the judge on the first day of April in the year of Our Lord 1756.

We were brought in an open cart from the Castle Gaol, along with a known housebreaker, Benjamin Munckman, and my poor friend Betty. It was a common sight for the prison cart to pass through the streets of York, and yet the crowd stopped to stare at Thomas Hague, who was notorious inland as well as up and down the coast.

Hague stared down at the market people – farmers from out of town, butchers and cheese-makers, drapers, goldsmiths and innkeepers – nodding a greeting to an acquaintance here, issuing a curse there to the soldiers we met on our way. He said nothing to me as we were taken down from the cart and led into the courthouse.

All this while I tried to follow Mally's advice and to keep a brave face, though I trembled from the cold. Besides, I knew I cut a poor figure in my dirty and creased skirt and bodice, and my unwashed linen. My hair was hanging in wisps over my pale, thin face, my eyes shadowed by lack of sleep.

Moreover, I could scarcely believe what was happening to me as we were taken before the judge. Here was I, Maggie Nightingale, who had until this day lived by a warm hearth with good food in my stomach and a father to protect me, now flung before a stranger who would decide whether I would live or die. And what a stranger was the man who sat high on the judge's bench staring down at me!

Mr Robert Carr was an ancient, stooping man with a lined face and crooked hands which played constantly on the surface of the desk in front of him. His fingers tapped as the Counsel for the King laid out the case. They fiddled with the papers and dusty leather volumes piled high before him and flew here and there with irritation at events.

'Speak up!' Justice Carr croaked at the King's Counsel. 'Make haste!' he yelled at Mr Peacock who gave witness that he had been present at the arrest of Thomas Hague and Maggie Nightingale, the prisoners in the dock.

I stared at Mr Peacock, silently begging him to speak up for me. But he avoided my gaze and gave only the facts – how his riding officer, Charles Howard, had first spied the Dutch vessel, the *Eagle*, hovering off shore late in the afternoon of March the twentieth, and how he, James Peacock, had suspected the accused,

Thomas Hague, of being in league with the ship's captain to bring unlicensed goods into port.

'Yes, yes!' Mr Carr barked sharply. 'What of the arrest, Mr Peacock?'

My heart sank as the exciseman firmly included me and my father in the account of events, drawing in the names of Hart and Penny as further accomplices and describing the moment shortly after dawn the next day when he and the militia had carried out the arrest.

'Did the villains resist?' the judge demanded.

'Aye, sir,' Peacock replied. 'Hague was armed with a scaning knife. The girl kicked and bit the men.'

'Enough!' said the judge, glaring at me and letting his restless hands fly to his white wig which he tugged more firmly on to his head. 'What other witnesses?' he asked the clerk of the court.

It was then that I first looked round the room and made out Mally sitting in the gallery, together with a neighbour, old Mary Goodnight, who I would see on her step each night baiting the lines for the next day's catch. I latched on to the faces of the two women as the only friends I had in the world. Mally smiled bravely and this made me raise my head a little higher to face the judge.

And now Luke Crispin came into the court, dragging his feet and muttering in a low voice that he had seen Hague and an accomplice named Ned Bonnet, now dead, together with Maggie Nightingale, sneak up Saltersgate in the dead of night, carrying their smuggled cargo into the Anchor Inn.

'You have no doubt about the girl?' Mr Carr interrupted.

Luke looked as though he would hesitate, and my heart beat fast for a few moments. I looked to Mally with a gleam of hope in my eyes.

But then Luke altered his mind and said that he was sure I was amongst the group of smugglers, and that my father had waited at the inn door to give us shelter.

And so it seemed all up with us, until Hague stood up to his full height, which was over six feet, and demanded to call witnesses of his own. This sent Mr Carr's fingers into a flurry of impatience. 'Make haste!' he ordered the clerk, as if his hands could hardly refrain from signing the death warrants.

The clerk went out but soon returned. 'Witnesses for the defence, namely Jim Penny and Solomon Hart, are nowhere to be found,' he announced. 'They were here five minutes ago until Mr Peacock mentioned their names in this case, but now they have fled.'

'Like rats from a sinking ship,' the judge remarked with the ghost of a smile, making notes upon a paper.

I saw Hague's face darken like thunder. The scar across his forehead seemed more livid, his brows knitted and he swore vengeance on the cowards who had deserted him.

'What have you to say in your own defence?' Mr Carr demanded.

Hague met his gaze. 'It is very hard upon me, my Lord, because, without witnesses, I am not properly prepared.'

'Why not? You knew the time of the assizes as well as I.' Making Hague stand back, the judge abruptly called my name. 'And you, Mistress Nightingale,' he quizzed, 'what words do you have to say to this court?'

This was worse than any torment I could imagine – to stand before a hanging judge who already thought me guilty and to speak up for myself. My throat was dry and narrow, my heart thumping hard at my chest as I stood up. But Mally's steady gaze drew me on.

'My father is dead,' I told the judge, my voice growing stronger as I gave my story. 'Else he would stand and tell you that I am a girl who wishes no one harm, who does no wrong except that forced upon me.'

'Who *forces* you to do wrong?' the judge demanded, tapping at his pile of books upon the word.

'Thomas Hague, Ned Bonnet and the rest,' I replied, quaking in my shoes, for Hague stood not two feet away. 'Terror stalks the streets when they are in town. They talk of dead men walking to make honest folk keep indoors. They use knives and pistols to rule over us!'

'Well said, Maggie!' Mally cried from the gallery.

'Yet you rowed out to the *Eagle* in their company,' Judge Carr pointed out.

'Only because I feared Tom Hague,' I argued. I felt my knees tremble under the judge's harsh gaze. How cruel it is to tell the truth to ears that will not hear.

Judge Carr contemplated me for fully five seconds. 'Do not take me for a fool, though this is All Fools' Day!' he snapped, before ordering me to stand down. 'The girl is a liar and a thief,' he said to the King's Counsel. 'She fought alongside Hague to escape arrest.'

I thought my heart should stop at this, and half wished it, for then at least my agony should be over. I saw Mally in the gallery put a hand to her mouth, felt Hague reach out and force me to stand upright as Judge Carr delivered his verdict.

'Thomas Hague and Maggie Nightingale, your country has found you guilty of a crime worthy of death. It is my office to pronounce sentence against you, and I say you shall be taken from this place and at a time to be decided, you shall indeed be hanged by the neck until you are dead. And may God have mercy upon you.'

Seven

All was confusion. I have no memory of being taken from that court, or of saying farewell to Mally, who it seems ran down from the gallery and threw herself upon me and had to be dragged away by the clerk of the court.

I saw only darkness ahead of me, heard only an echoing wave of gasps and cries surround me, was dimly aware of Betty by my side, weeping for her own fate, which was to be the same as mine.

We rode through the streets to the gaol without me coming to my senses and were thrown into the condemned cell, apart from the common criminals whose company we had kept until now.

Here we huddled together without bed or straw to lie upon – Betty and I the only females in a wretched group of eight men, and both of us too confounded to speak or comfort one another.

A condemned man approached Hague with a hollow grin. He slapped him on the back and said he could not believe it was all up with the most notorious of smugglers it had ever been his pleasure to meet.

'Who says that all is up with me?' Hague snarled back, wresting himself free of the man and straightening the buttoned cuffs of his fine jacket. 'It is not over until the hangman tightens the knot.'

At this poor Betty cried out for mercy and fell upon the filthy floor. Ignoring her, Hague strode to the cell door and rattled at the iron bars. 'Gaoler, bring me brandy!' he cried, as if intending to drink himself into oblivion without a care for the misery he had bestowed on others.

The gaoler came – a short, stout man dressed in a leather apron, with great keys about his waist. He pushed a jug of brandy through the bars then took payment with a knowing wink. But before he could pocket his money and turn on his heel, Hague reached through the bars and took hold of his wrist.

'Stay and drink with me!' he said. 'I have need of company in this miserable hell-hole.'

I could see that this was not the man's custom but that he perceived in Hague a source of rich pickings in the days to come.

Indeed, Hague encouraged him in this notion. 'I will reward you well,' he promised, holding up his left hand to display a thick gold ring on his finger. 'And I have money besides.'

Being a greedy man, the gaoler soon complied. He took one of the large keys and turned it in the lock, waiting for Hague and the other prisoners to stand well back before he pushed open the door and entered.

'Welcome!' Hague greeted him with a flourish then handed around the jug of brandy, which was seized eagerly by all the condemned men. Betty and I huddled in a far corner, holding each other in silence, for we could not frame words to express the fear which gripped us.

'Drink!' Hague invited the gaoler, coolly proceeding to make arrangements with the man for his own funeral. 'You will hire four men as my mourners,' he instructed, 'and I will give you three pounds to be shared among them. You will make sure to buy me a neat coffin and see that all is done properly thereafter.'

The man drank and nodded. 'And what is to be my payment?' he demanded.

'You may take this ring from my finger and this coat from my back,' Hague replied, forcing more brandy on him.

I shuddered meanwhile, wondering who would attend my coffin and make sure that I had a Christian burial.

The other men in the condemned cell fell quiet, perhaps sharing my thoughts.

The drinking continued for some time and the conversation turned to lighter subjects as Hague recalled the goods he had smuggled and the profits he had made. 'I have seven ankers of gin stowed away on Westerdale Moor,' he boasted, 'together with five parcels of tobacco and four canisters of finest Bohea tea!'

The greedy gaoler's eyes glinted as he calculated how he might lay his hands on Hague's store once the villain was dead.

'Drink!' Hague commanded, thrusting the jug at him. Then he turned to me and my heart all but stopped dead, for I rightly guessed that he would draw me into the centre of things.

'I will not sing!' I told him before he asked. 'You have dragged me down into hell with you and I will no longer do your bidding!'

This caused some laughter among the condemned men, who took notice of me for the first time.

'Why have you done this?' I implored Hague, keeping my distance and not caring who heard us. 'I have never harmed you.'

Hague looked steadily at me through narrowed eyes. 'Poor Maggie,' he sighed without meaning it. Then under his breath he added, 'You may yet be useful to me.'

At least the villain seemed to have forgotten his intention to make me sing. Instead, he turned to ply the gaoler with more brandy, boasting again of all he owned – namely three fine horses also kept on Westerdale Moor, two silver pistols and a feathered hat made by the finest hatter in London.

The gaoler nodded and laughed, promising Hague that his secrets would be safe with him and asking whether or not Hague had any family on whom he might confer the wealth.

'None!' Hague declared, slapping the man's back and sliding his arm around his shoulder. 'I have neither wife, nor brother or sister still living.'

The gaoler swayed and smiled happily. He clapped his own arm around Hague's waist and said that for his part he hoped the hangman would do his job well and that the end would come quick, for Hague was a good-hearted fellow even though he had been a smuggler all his life.

I listened with disgust, noting that the other men in the cell had fallen quiet and stopped drinking some time before. They watched and waited, all eyes fixed on the drunken gaoler.

Hague waited too. He gave the foolish man the last of the drink, making as if to do a merry dance with him across the filthy floor. The gaoler laughed and half toppled against the wall as Hague released him, and before he could pull himself upright, four of the men fell heavily upon him, striking out with fists and feet.

'Stand back!' cried the drunken man, rolling helplessly under their kicks.

I gasped as I saw him go down. Betty sprang to her feet and cried out.

'Hush!' Hague warned savagely, watching the men do their work until the gaoler lay senseless.

Then Hague sprang forward and wrested the great ring of keys from the man's belt, held back the other men who clamoured for them, ran to the cell door and found the one that would turn in the lock.

I stared at the bloodied man lying on the ground, making no sound. I felt no pity, only fear at what Hague was about, and with it a flicker of hope in my fast-beating heart.

The door was open at last. Men ran silently from the condemned cell like filthy scarecrows suddenly come alive, fleeing down the arched stone passageway that led past other cells, seizing back their lives.

'Come!' Hague told me, taking me by the arm.

Without a thought I grabbed Betty, who crouched in terror on the floor. I dragged her with me as Hague made his escape.

'What about us? Remember us!' the ragged creatures cried from their cells, stretching their arms through the bars.

Hague flung the keys at them, letting them fight and tear at each other in a frenzy. 'The more the merrier!' he cried, turning down a side passage that had light at the end of it.

Soon the whole prison was filled with escaping men and women, bringing soldiers running from corridors and rooms above our heads, armed with guns and bayonets. The first shot was fired, rapid orders shouted.

'This way!' Hague decided, dragging me further from the main struggle into passages that ran like a warren under the ground.

I kept hold of Betty, who was gasping and faint. 'Have courage!' I begged.

She rallied and staggered on.

Behind us gunshot echoed, men cried and groaned.

We fled like rats underground, turning and twisting, darting away whenever we saw the red coats of the soldiers, running for our lives.

Twice Hague came face to face with a soldier. The first one aimed his gun and fired wide, giving Hague time to throw himself at him and wrestle him to the ground. He seized the man's gun and struck him with the butt, trampling on him, then stealing a knife from his belt and running on with Betty and me.

The second time we came upon the soldier from behind and Hague was armed. He quickly plunged the knife into the soldier's back and once more stepped over him as if his life were nothing.

'Leave me. I can't go on!' Betty sobbed.

But I would not abandon her. 'Run!' I told her, putting my arm around her waist. I followed Hague up stone stairs, around corners until we came to a large room with low windows overlooking the street.

Behind us was terror and darkness. Before us was the bright light of day.

Hague took one look before seizing a chair and dashing it against the window. There was a crash and then the glass shattered into a thousand shining splinters. Hague struck again, loosening the frame from the window then pulling it free. 'Jump!' he ordered.

I ran to the window with Betty and looked down. The drop was not more than a yard on to the street below, so I pushed her forward and made her leap first. I soon followed, and then Hague.

On the street there was more confusion. Passers-by had gathered in a large crowd by the gate of the prison and saw us leap to freedom. Some made way for us, either in fright or because they pitied us; others stood before us, pushing us back and calling for the soldiers.

Then someone recognised Hague. 'Stand out of his way!' the man cried, pushing others aside. 'If you value your lives or those of your family, you will not cross Thomas Hague!'

The warning was heeded. Suddenly our opponents fell back and we ran quickly across the street down one of the small alleyways and thence up some steps on to the broad walkway around the top of the old city walls. Seeing that we were not pursued for the moment, Hague paused for breath.

This was my chance, as I thought. Though my lungs were bursting, I spied more steps down to the ground and thrust Betty towards them.

Hague saw my plan and dragged me back. 'Let the girl go,' he snarled, 'but you must stay!'

I struggled and kicked. 'Run!' I cried to Betty, who seemed dazed and unable to move. 'This is your chance. You must leave me!'

Her dark eyes stared back at me, brimming with tears.

'Go to your mother and your brothers and sisters!' I whispered, unable to escape Hague's grasp.

And so Betty turned and fled down the steps into the narrow streets below.

And that was the last I ever saw of my prison friend.

'We will live as new people in a new world!' Hague announced to the poor company around the supper table at Gin Garth.

It was the night of our escape, after we had fled the prison along the city walls and come down at last into a back street where Hague knew of a safe house. The woman there had hidden us well for an hour or more, sending for horses and providing us each with a change of clothes. By four o'clock we were in the saddle, heading eastwards out of town, intent on reaching the open moor by nightfall.

None pursued us, though we heard from other travellers that five men had died in the riot at the gaol and that the gaoler himself was unlikely to live through the night.

Breathing fresh air into my stifled lungs, I had ridden silently beside my companion, wondering where we were bound.

The answer was soon clear. On the top of the moor, almost within sight of the sea, Hague turned his horse down a track which soon grew narrow and overgrown. Bracken and brambles caught in our horses' feet and tugged at my new crimson skirt, and soon we must dismount to proceed on foot.

'Where are we going?' I protested, feeling that my legs would scarcely carry me after the events of the day. Condemned to death in the morning and now walking free in the company of my worst enemy, I set one feeble foot in front of the other.

'To a new life!' Hague had replied heartily, leading me to a hidden cottage surrounded by heather bushes and hawthorn trees. 'Prepare for a long journey, Maggie, for our days in Old England are at an end.'

And so he said to our host, a man named Old Zag who lived in the cottage and kept careful guard over the smuggled goods brought here by pack-horse in the dead of night. His wife Isabel, as old and gnarled as he, helped in this trade by dividing tobacco into smaller parcels and by decanting liquor into stone bottles.

'We will live where nobody can blame us for our past, where none know us and where the noose will not hang over us with every step we take!'

'What do you mean?' I cried. I had never seen

Hague's eyes glitter so – with excitement instead of hatred.

Old Zag gave a low laugh. 'Are you a good sailor?' he asked, thrusting a plate loaded with boiled beef and potatoes at me. His hair was long and bushy, like a thatched roof; his clothes smelled of smoke from the old chimney.

'Why? Where am I going?' Alarm rose within me. Home lay ten miles away, yet it seemed I was not to return there.

'To a new start, Maggie!' Hague proclaimed, standing up from the table and offering a toast.

Old Zag raised his tankard and Isabel smiled a toothless grin.

'But I wish to stay here where my home is,' I protested.

Hague shook his head. 'Nowhere is safe to you now, child. Everywhere you go in Yorkshire, aye in the whole of England, there is a warrant out for your arrest to make you keep your date with the hangman.'

'But I did nothing wrong! They would not hang me.'

Hague fixed me with a cold stare. 'They would hang you until you are dead, as readily as they would hang me,' he insisted. 'Believe me, Maggie, I saved your life this afternoon.'

'No, you have ruined it!' I cried, pushing away my plate and retreating to a corner of the small, dark room.

'Tut!' the old woman cried, throwing scraps to a half-starved dog lurking by the door. 'I would leave the ungrateful wretch to her fate, Mister Hague.'

'Except that she is useful to me,' he argued. He took out his pipe, filled it with tobacco and lit it. 'We must take on a new name apiece, Maggie, to fit us for our new life.'

'What name? Where are we going?'

'You will be Annie. I will be Richard Butler, a gentleman farmer. And when people ask, we will say that I am your father and you are my daughter, joined by blood in a tie that none may break.'

'My father?' I stammered, unable to believe my ears.

'It is a good plan,' Old Zag muttered. 'The soldiers will not look for a father and daughter.'

I shook my head and tried to run out of the house, but I had not got six steps beyond the door when Hague caught up with me and turned me to face him.

He stooped low, bringing his gaze level with mine, fixing me with eyes more grey and more cruel than the sea itself. 'Tomorrow we begin our journey to London,' he told me. 'We ride with care, telling no one who we are, only that I am a gentleman taking his daughter to stay with her aunt in Hampstead. No one will suspect.'

I stared back at him, my heart fluttering, my breath coming short.

'But we will not linger long in the capital. I will secure passage on a ship.'

Hague paused to let me take in this news, then spoke a sentence that was to seal my fate. 'This time next week we will set sail for the New World.'

I sank down amongst the heather in dread. As Hague towered over me and the black sky opened up behind him with never a star to light my way, I realised what this meant.

We were to sail for the New World, not as convicts, but as free men. We were to cross the wide ocean together and never return.

And so events were set. And now, though I was not to die on the gallows alongside Thomas Hague, yet I feared with a sinking heart that I was condemned to live with the villain for the rest of my natural life!

Part Two

One

In all my life I had never travelled further than the city of York. I knew the fishing village of Staithes to the north and had ridden one summer Sunday with my father to Hull in the south. But of the wider world I was ignorant.

I had only the haziest of notions of London, where I headed with Thomas Hague on that Friday in early April.

I knew that the King lived in a great palace there and that the streets were thronged with people who did not know each other and who hurried about their business with closed faces and no words of friendship between them. There was great wealth there, I believed, and wide streets with carriages, though I heard that many wretches lived in the gutter and stole what they could to put food into their mouths.

'Remember!' my tormentor told me as we set forth at dawn on that Friday morning. 'I will not answer to the name of Thomas Hague, but that of Richard

Butler. And henceforth you are Annie Butler, my dear daughter and a young lady of manners.'

I scowled in the early light, forced to sit sideways in the saddle with my skirt and cloak arranged modestly around me. My horse was a sturdy chestnut mare with a bad temper who kept snatching at the reins to lower her head and graze on the grass at the roadside. Hague, or Butler as I shall now call him, rode a tall bay gelding who stepped out strongly.

It was Butler's plan that we should be clear of York before breakfast, and sure enough we soon left behind the streets and houses, making good progress through open countryside before most folk were out of their beds. The grey dawn strengthened into full sunlight, with a clear sky above and sprigs of spring green in the hedgerows to either side.

I breathed deep, reminding myself that yesterday I was condemned to die, and yet now I rode free. And though I was not grateful to Butler, I did give thanks to a greater power, which is the Lord above. For to be out of the stinking gaol and from under the shadow of the gallows was the greatest relief to be imagined.

Butler himself was in high spirits. He bade cheerful good mornings to farmers driving their carts out to the fields and to a gentleman traveller heading north on the road we travelled.

The gentleman nodded back, looking a little

curiously at the two of us, trying to make out from our clothes what rank in society we might hold.

'Do you travel to York?' Butler asked, striking up a conversation while I sat and let my horse graze.

'Aye, to meet with a clergyman of my acquaintance there.' The gentleman cocked his head to one side. 'I hear news of a riot in the city yesterday. Do you know anything of what took place?'

My companion did not hesitate. 'Aye,' he replied. 'It began in the gaol and spilled out into the streets. They say five were killed and many desperate ruffians escaped!'

I grew nervous at this, but the gentleman merely nodded. 'Well, I must look to my own safety as I draw near the city,' he decided, pressing his horse on.

'Do!' Butler urged. 'As for myself and my daughter here, I shall be glad when we are safe out of reach of the villains!'

With this we continued on our way, Butler smiling to himself and I breathing a sigh of relief, until we came to an inn by the roadside, where Butler dismounted and called for a man to take his horse.

'Come, Annie,' he instructed, handing me down from my mare. 'Do not stoop and cower away so!' he hissed as he led me into the inn. 'You must act like a lady, or I will do the hangman's job for him and strangle the breath out of you!'

Well, I was no lady and had little idea of how to act

like one, but as I was in fear of my life, I made a good attempt. I held my head up and resolved to stay silent, in case my homely way of speaking betrayed me.

The landlord brought us ham to break our fast. He and Butler talked of the news from York, how many of the villains had been recaptured during the night, and laughing between them about the foolish gaoler who had been tricked by the notorious smuggler, Thomas Hague, and who now lay close to death for his pains.

At this I started and almost choked.

'Hague will lie low in York for a week or more,' was Butler's opinion. 'He will not venture forth until the news has grown stale and the soldiers have dispersed.'

Our landlord agreed. He told Butler that he had a very pretty daughter and must take good care of me. 'There are villains everywhere,' he warned. 'Cutpurses roam the countryside. Highwaymen ply their trade between here and London.'

'I will keep her safe,' Butler promised, paying the landlord in coins that I guessed were counterfeit. 'She is to visit her aunt in Hampstead while I conduct business in the city.'

And so we were on our way again, playing the innocents, buoyed up by the goodwill of those we cheated, until the horses grew stale and we must stop in a small market town near the border of Lincolnshire.

Here Butler took me through the streets to a house

belonging to a woman he knew, who was introduced to me as the governess.

Now it was clear to me that the lessons the woman taught were not honest, for she was tightly corseted and wearing a low bodice, with gold around her neck and paint on her face to disguise the wrinkles about her eyes and mouth. She greeted Butler silently and listened carefully to the instructions he gave her.

'First, you must provide us with clean linen and a change of clothes for the girl, made by a good seamstress.'

The governess took hold of me and turned me around. 'How old is she?' she asked.

'Eleven, perhaps twelve,' Butler guessed.

'I am thirteen!' I retorted.

'Not well grown,' the woman said, as if I were one of the vegetables that sprouted in the flat fields around there. 'She will need a silk bodice and a satin skirt.'

'And a hat?' Butler asked, evidently already bored by the task of turning me into a lady. He said he must go out on business of his own and ordered the governess to keep me always in her sight. 'I need the girl with me while I secure a passage on board a ship that will carry me to the New World,' he explained, showing the governess the gold coins he would pay her for her pains. 'A daughter is the best disguise for a man fleeing for his life, and so we must turn her out well.'

The woman promised to carry off the task, taking

me to an upstairs room and bidding me take off my clothes.

I said I would not while she waited in the room. She said she would not leave, for she did not trust me alone. 'You will jump from the window and flee when my back is turned,' she muttered.

'And where would I run?' I retorted. 'I know no one in this town and I am many miles from home!'

At which I pretended to break down in tears to make her relent, since I did indeed plan to jump through the window into the street below.

But the old woman did not melt. Again she bade me undress to my cotton shift, bringing stockings and pure white linen from a cupboard and then a skirt of pink satin topped by a bodice of pale green silk with pink rosebuds embroidered in a panel down the front. Pretty green ribbons were threaded through the lace at my neck to match the ribbons in the hat which the governess gave me, and though my state was desperate, I gave a gasp of pleasure when she presented me to the mirror in the corner of the room.

'Well?' the woman asked.

I stared at my reflection, seeing a trim figure adorned with ribbons and lace, wearing a stylish straw hat to one side of her head, on top of dark brown hair all plaited and curled. I said nothing, but I could not help smiling and turning this way and that.

Soon Butler returned and told us he had bought

places on the overnight coach to London. 'You will travel in style,' he informed me, looking less happy than I had expected at my transformation. He paid the governess five guineas for her trouble and swore her to secrecy. 'We were not here. You have not seen us,' he insisted. 'There are soldiers in town who are likely to come knocking at your door.'

The old woman gave her promise. 'And will I never see you again?' she asked, taking hold of Butler's arm to detain him. 'Will you send news from the New World?'

He pulled away. 'No tears!' he insisted. 'We cannot know the future, but be glad that I have escaped the gallows and ask me no more!'

And so I understood that he meant more to the old woman than he had told me, and I looked more closely and saw perhaps his long, sharp features in hers, and thought with a shock that this was Butler's mother, who was saying goodbye to him for evermore.

It is a cruel man who can walk away from the woman who bore him without a backward glance, even though I, who was nothing to her, looked back and saw that she stood on her doorstep and wept.

We took the overnight coach, me seated inside, Butler riding on top with the coachman and guard who sat upon the mail box with a blunderbuss across his knees. At first I said nothing to my fellow passengers – two gentlemen and a lady who befriended me and gave me pastries, for she said I looked thin. When she asked me about my business in London and about my parents, I answered with few words, affecting shyness and then sleep.

'Poor motherless child,' the woman sighed to the man who sat next to her. 'A girl just entering womanhood needs a mother to guide her.'

'Aye, and the father seems unkind,' the husband said, referring to Butler and thinking I was asleep. 'He has a hard face.'

At which I longed to spring up from my seat and confess everything and have these good people take me under their wing, except that I knew I could not risk the hangman's noose and that I was, as I have said, tied to my tormentor by a bond I could not break.

So we travelled through the night, rocked by the motion of the coach, plunging downhill and straining up the slopes, stopping twice to change our team of horses. During all this time Butler did not exchange a word with me, but kept his eyes and ears open, suspecting every shadow on the roadside.

At last the dawn light appeared in the east. Talk among the other passengers told me that we were within twenty miles of London.

'My bones ache with this shaking and rattling,' the lady complained. 'I shall be glad when this journey is done!'

Her husband yawned. The other gentleman dipped

into his waistcoat pocket and drew out a gold watch.

It was then that we heard the sound of galloping hooves and men's voices commanding us to stop.

'It is highwaymen!' the lady cried, shrinking against her husband's broad chest.

Startled, I leaned out of the window along with the man with the watch. We saw three men in red coats.

'Soldiers!' the man said. 'Stay calm, madam. We are not in danger.'

Aye, but we are! I said to myself, fearing discovery. I heard the coachman call for the horses to halt and saw the guard jump down from his seat to fix the iron brake shoe to the back wheel.

At last we stopped and the soldiers rode up to us. They ordered us down from the coach.

'What is the matter?' the man with the watch demanded, angry at the delay.

'We have orders to inspect all passengers on this highway and the goods you carry,' the soldier in charge explained. He cast a weary eye over me, Butler, the lady and her husband, plus the irate gentleman. 'Who does the girl belong to?' he asked.

Butler stepped forward, a false, brazen smile on his thin face, the brim of his hat pulled well down to hide the scar on his forehead. He put his arm around my shoulder. 'My name is Richard Butler and this is my daughter, Annie.'

I held my breath as the soldier studied us, taking in

my silk skirt and pretty hat, together with my white stockings and shoes of green leather.

'Where did you board this coach?' the sergeant asked.

Butler named the town and said that he owned an estate outside Lincoln and that we travelled to London to see his sister. 'The child is weary and longs for the comforts of her aunt's house,' my so-called father said.

'Aye, and the mail is delayed while you keep us here,' the guard pointed out to the soldiers. 'I will pay dear if it is delivered late to London.'

'Let us get on our way,' the man with the watch urged. 'It is a cold dawn, and I have business in the docks with a merchantman from the West Indies.'

The soldiers left off looking at us then and searched the coach. Butler kept tight hold of me all this while and for my part I scarcely breathed.

After what seemed an age the search was over. 'You may drive on,' the sergeant told the coachman, still with a wary eye on me and Butler.

With much muttering and grumbling we resumed our places in the coach. The coachman took up the reins, the guard took off the brake and we were ready to go.

The soldiers mounted their horses. 'Watch out for villains as you ride into town,' the sergeant warned. 'You know there was a riot in the prison at York and we suspect that the convicts may head south.'

The lady passenger clung tight to her husband at this, while I sank back into the corner and dared not raise my eyes from the ground.

But Butler loudly thanked the sergeant and said that we would look out, but we were not afraid, for the guard carried a gun that would see off any desperate man.

Then the coachman flicked his whip and the horses went forward along the straight road to London. And when I gathered courage to lean out of the window and look back, the road behind us was empty and the sun had risen over the horizon into a clear blue sky.

Two

London. The mere name overwhelms me still, though I have voyaged across the ocean and seen more of the world than I ever imagined.

London, England's great capital city, divided by the mighty Thames, home to a million lost and blighted souls.

I remember that my spirit shrank as I entered those streets for the first time. I looked out from the coach that fine Saturday morning on scenes of such filth and meanness as I can barely describe.

Houses jostled and tumbled against each other, their roofs almost touching, their chimney stacks crumbling, their gutters running with foul water. Men pushed carts laden with foodstuffs and wood for burning, women cried out their wares. A butcher hacked the head off the carcase of a beast hanging outside his door. A blind beggar craved alms from a clergyman who brushed him aside into the gutter.

And everywhere there was noise and confusion – children running after geese that strayed from the alleys into the main thoroughfare, men climbing ladders with bundles of straw to repair leaking roofs, women standing gossiping in doorways, tanners curing skins, cobblers mending shoes, serving girls running errands and carrying parcels from drapers' to coopers', to bookshop and on.

I blocked my ears with my hands as the coach crawled through the crowds and tried not to see what I could not bear – shivering children with hollow eyes and empty bellies wandering aimlessly, a crippled woman in rags lying across the doorway to a church.

'Have courage, Annie,' my lady companion said gently. 'Your father will soon take you to your aunt's house, far from here, where the grass grows green and you may freely breathe the air.'

My stomach had turned and I felt sick at the sights I saw.

We stopped at last in the midst of the melee, outside an inn close to the great river. Here we said farewell to our fellow travellers, the lady being sad to see me go and promising she should come to Hampstead to visit me if we would but give her our address. But my 'father', as I am forced to call him, invented a name and so I knew I would never see her more.

After this, Butler and I made off down to the wharf, which was stacked with baskets of recently unloaded fish. The smell here was familiar to me, and for a moment I felt at ease, seeing the fishermen work with their scaning knives, slitting the fish along the belly, gutting them and preparing them for market. We did not stop long, however, for Butler was in search of lodgings close to the water, from where he could venture out to find us passage to the New World.

'You will find rooms above the carpenter's shop down Cooper's Yard,' one of the fishermen informed us, not bothering to take the pipe from his mouth. 'The beds are not as soft or as clean as you might like, but the food is ample and whatever secrets you bear with you will be kept close as the grave!'

Another man laughed at this, but I soon found out the source of the joke, since we went along and discovered that the carpenter's trade was principally in making coffins, which stood outside the door, lined up like so many sentry boxes. The man's name was Samuel Goodnight, which made even Butler stretch his thin lips in what might be taken for a smile.

'The customers you serve must make their final "Goodnight" when they depart from here in those fine caskets!' he joked.

The carpenter smiled wearily back. 'You are not the first to say so,' he muttered, taking coins from Butler and testing them between his teeth. 'Your mattresses are made of straw and you must check them for rats before you sleep,' he warned.

Butler swore and said it was the man's job to chase

out the rats, not his, if he paid good money for the beds, which of course he did not.

And so a bargain was made and we trudged up the stairs to find a room bare of all furniture except for two simple beds and a plain table made from the same light wood as the coffins below.

The room looked out over the river, which flowed sluggishly to my eye and carried with it much flotsam, as well as the small rowing-boats which the fishermen used to bring in their catch. On the distant south bank I saw more houses and wharves, with some sailing ships moored, and as I looked to right and left, the city stretched as far as the eye could see.

'Make yourself at home, Annie!' Butler said to me with his dry laugh. 'And have no fear. The militiamen are as likely to find us here as they are to find a needle in a haystack!'

I felt this to be true. And it followed therefore that if I were to flee from Butler into the warren of London streets, he might never find me out. I would wait until he slept, seize my moment and run!

But the devil saw the thought flash through my eyes. He came up to me and thrust his face close to mine, swearing that if I ever tried to escape him, he would follow and slit my throat. 'Besides,' he said, 'I am not such a fool as to let you out of my sight!'

I sighed and hid my face behind my hands. 'You will be punished for this!' I cried.

'Who will punish me?' he laughed.

I was beside myself and spoke heedlessly. 'God will! You are a sinner and God will punish you!'

'For what, Annie? For taking you and dressing you in fine clothes and making a lady of you? For travelling across the world with you and providing you with the means to live in the great cabin of a mighty ship, sitting at table with the captain and at last landing in Virginia to begin a new life?'

'For ruining me and bringing me under the shadow of the gallows!' I cried out.

'Hush!' Butler stopped my mouth with his hand. 'Mr Goodnight is at work below. We don't want him to overhear our business!'

I was quiet then. In any case, my captor had given me much to think about.

He said we were to sail in a large ship to Virginia, which was a place unknown to me, though I knew of Greenland where the whaling boats sailed, where mountains of ice floated in the green sea.

As it says in the song I sang often by my father's hearth,

> 'We never was downhearted
> Nor let our courage fail
> But bore away up to Greenland
> For to catch the Greenland whale.'

This made me think again of my home town. I saw in my mind's eye the steep, narrow streets and the steps leading to the ruined abbey. I smelled the fish on the wharves and heard the chatter of the flither pickers as they passed by my father's door.

And lastly I thought of this real father, now buried under the earth beside the sailors and fishermen, the boat makers and the scaning women, on the slope of St Mary's churchyard, overlooking the wide sea.

Butler's plan was to sleep through the Saturday and to go that night in search of a ship. This could be done by frequenting the inns along the Thames towards Deptford Reach, where the merchant ships bound for America were moored.

These inns were darker and dirtier than the Anchor, filled with the stench of tobacco smoke and crowded with sailors of every race, colour and creed. I went with Butler from one to another, astonished by the babble of foreign tongues and somewhat afraid. He, however, played the man of the world, asking the innkeepers if they knew of a good ship about to set sail for the American colonies, inquiring about the captain and letting it be known that he had the means to pay for the best cabin and a seat at the captain's table.

At last we came to a place where the innkeeper named a ship called the *Good Endeavour*, docked nearby. 'Captain Andrews comes here nightly to dine,' he promised. 'His ship trades in tobacco and other goods. I believe he is to set sail from here tomorrow and then to drop anchor at Bugby's Hole to lay in fresh provisions.'

Butler pricked up his ears at this and sat me down at a table near the window overlooking the wharf. 'Tomorrow is earlier than I had planned,' he told me. 'I must buy a sea chest and make preparations!'

He seemed anxious among the sailors, perhaps fearing that he might be recognised, even though we were far from home. So he watched and listened and kept his distance, waiting for the captain to arrive.

Captain Andrews came at last, accompanied by two other men – one small and lithe, with thick dark hair tied back from his brown face, the other tall with a bald head and all the brawn of a blacksmith, with thick forearms, broad shoulders and sturdy legs. The captain himself was taller still, but more slight, standing very erect and casting a careful eye around the inn to see what company he kept.

'There's our man!' Butler said the moment he saw the captain, observing him to decide if he liked what he saw.

I too watched as the three men sat down at the next table and ordered their food and drink. I warmed to the small man's ready smile, but shrank away from the sturdy one, who did not smile or talk, but merely scowled at anyone who caught his gaze. The captain himself seemed distant and reserved.

Butler waited impatiently until they had finished their meal then approached their table. He went straight to business. 'I hear you set sail for America,' he began.

'Aye, within the week,' the captain confirmed.

'I wish to secure passage for me and my daughter,' Butler said, gesturing towards me. 'Her poor mother died of a fever some two months back. It is our desire to start a new life in a new world.'

The captain studied me for a few moments. 'What is her name?'

'Annie. And I am Richard Butler, from the county of Lincolnshire. Annie is my only living relative, and a very dear daughter to me.'

I cursed him inwardly for such dishonesty in playing upon the captain's sympathy. And yet I could see that he seemed very sincere, and so must admire him at the same time.

'There is space for two in the great cabin,' Captain Andrews said thoughtfully. 'You would take your place with the other passengers.'

I frowned at the thought of spending several weeks in the close company of strangers and was glad when Butler said he wished for two small cabins and agreed a price of fifteen guineas for each. Other arrangements were made upon the spot, hands were shaken and Captain Andrews called for Madeira wine.

'Come!' The captain called for me to join them, sitting me down by his side and opposite the members of his crew who I now knew to be Bill Carthy, the ship's boatswain, and the older of the two, Dick Trapp, the ship's mate.

'How do you do, Mistress Butler?' the captain asked, excessively polite, which caused Bill Carthy to wink at me and smile.

'I do very well, thank you, sir,' I replied with a blush.

'And should you like to sail with us to America?'

'I should, sir.'

'And you shouldn't regret leaving England behind?'

A quick glance told me that Butler was listening to every word. 'I should not, sir,' I whispered faintly, not being as good a liar as my captor.

'Her sadness is for her mother,' Butler broke in. 'But she has a brave heart and will soon forget.'

Captain Andrews shook his head at this. 'A child never forgets. The loss lies deep as the ocean.'

At which I shed a sudden tear – for my true father, and not as they thought for my false mother. But I liked the captain we had met and tried to smile through my tears.

He told my false father that he must take me home to our lodgings and come again prepared to board the *Good Endeavour* at midday the next day. 'We will cast anchor at Bugby for one day to bring in provisions, then sail to Gravesend where we will take on board beef, mutton and pork. On Friday we sail for Virginia.'

Butler had to be content with this, though I knew he would have liked to see the last of England before then. He shook hands with the captain and we left the inn to make our way home to Cooper's Yard.

I slept above Goodnight's coffins that night, and if there were rats in the mattress they did not disturb me, for I was exhausted.

I woke at dawn to hear Butler in the yard below telling the carpenter that he had need of a big sea chest in which to transport our goods to the New World. Leaning out of the window, I saw Goodnight drag out a box made of plain oak and heard Butler instruct him to add a strong padlock, together with a secret drawer with lock and key. He then came upstairs and took out a leather bag from under his bed which he had brought with him on the coach journey from Lincolnshire. I watched him count out bank-notes on to the bed, together with gold coins, several gold watches, a dozen jewelled rings, and silver plate worth many hundreds of guineas.

I gasped at the sight, not knowing how many items were forged or how many genuine.

'You will need more clothes,' he told me, ignoring my surprise. 'We will buy them in Gravesend.'

The morning was spent then in calling out orders to

the carpenter above the clamour of a dozen church bells calling the righteous to worship. Butler sent out for brandy, sugar and lemons, linen for our beds, shoes for our feet, wax candles for our cabin and any number of items that would make our voyage comfortable. By mid-day the chest was well stocked and the precious items secreted in the locked compartment. A handcart came into the yard and the chest was loaded on to it.

'And so farewell,' Butler told Samuel Goodnight as he stood by the row of half made coffins in the yard. 'And if you ever sail to Virginia, be sure to ask for me there!'

The carpenter gave a grim smile. 'I make my living out of the dead,' he reminded us as he watched us on our way. 'I warrant there are more bodies to bury in this one great city alone than there are in the whole of the New World.'

Three

Heavy rain poured from the heavens as I set foot on board the *Good Endeavour* for the first time. It soaked the deck and dripped from the furled sails, driving into my face so that I must duck my head and trust that it would not blow me against the rails.

The boatswain, Bill Carthy, darted forward to steady me and lead me to my cabin, Butler leaving me to fend for myself as he went to seek out Captain Andrews. Carthy and I went below deck, down a narrow staircase, along an oak panelled corridor and into the smallest chamber I had ever seen.

'You must call this home for forty days,' Carthy said with a cheerful grin. 'Your father will take the cabin next door.'

'Forty days?' I echoed. 'Is the ocean so wide?'

'Wider than you can believe,' he assured me. 'But fear not, the *Endeavour* has sturdy sides to withstand the winds and storms we will encounter.'

'And shall I like Virginia?' I asked, looking round to see that my tiny room had no window and scarce enough space for a narrow bed and a chair. There was a sconce for a candle on one wall, a small, cracked looking glass on another.

The boatswain shrugged his shoulders. 'Are you like most young girls? Do you favour the streets of London with the noise and bustle, the carriages, the fashionable ladies and fine gentlemen?'

I quickly shook my head.

'Then you may like Virginia,' he said with another smile, closing the door upon me.

Left alone, I found that I might take three steps along the length of my cabin and but two steps across its width. However, I felt happy there, with four wooden walls around me and none to pry. I tried the bed and found the mattress soft. I had tried the chair and risked a look into the mirror before a knock came on my door and Butler's voice ordered me to join him up on deck. 'I see something that will interest you!' he promised.

So I gathered my damp cloak about me and followed him, squeezing past a man and a woman with a family of small children, all bound for the great cabin under the direction of Bill Carthy. On deck I soon spotted Butler among the bustle and made my way towards him.

But activity on the wharf stopped me in my tracks – a glimpse of red uniforms and rifles, the shouting of orders, the tramp of feet.

My heart missed a beat and I gripped the deck rail, putting a hand over my stomach to steady my breathing.

'Come!' Butler called, standing with his collar turned up and his hat pulled down.

I stumbled against a barrel, bumped into a pile of hempen sacks, then gave way to Dick Trapp carrying a roll of sailcloth across his shoulder before I finally reached Butler's side. 'Have the soldiers come for us?' I cried faintly.

'Hush!' His eyes glittered. 'Look again!'

This time I saw that the redcoats were marching a group of wretched men up the gangplank to board the *Endeavour*. The men wore chains around their ankles and wrists, their clothes were ragged and their faces covered in grime. Some coughed as they shuffled along, one turned and spat fiercely towards the wharf – his rough farewell to the country of his birth.

And I realised at once that these wretches were convicts sent for transportation to the colonies. I counted them, one, two, three . . . thirteen men in all, their wrists and ankles chafed by the irons, heads hanging as they were poked and prodded up the plank by the soldiers who guarded them.

Captain Andrews watched their arrival from his quarterdeck. 'Clap them under the hatches!' he ordered sternly.

The prisoners filed on deck then waited in the rain

and the wind while Trapp and another strong man lifted two wooden trapdoors which opened up on to a dark, stale space below.

The smell that emerged was foul and I could tell that the hold was not a fit place to keep animals, let alone men, whatever their crimes. Still I clutched my stomach and shrank from the sight of the redcoats.

'They have not come for you!' Butler laughed quietly at me, perhaps enjoying the notion that we ourselves had narrowly escaped such a fate, or worse. He strode brazenly on to the quarterdeck to demand why the captain had not told him about our fellow passengers the night before.

'Is it safe for my daughter to sail on a ship laden with convicts?' he asked in a loud voice as the prisoners were thrust into the dark hold.

One man glanced sideways at me as he disappeared from view, giving me an empty, hopeless stare, so that I felt ashamed of observing him, dressed in my finery, with my green velvet cloak about me.

'The convicts are kept under lock and key,' Captain Andrews assured my father. 'There is no danger to you, sir, or Mistress Annie. Besides, who would be your hewers of logs and fetchers of water if it were not for these wretches condemned to work as slaves in the New World?'

Butler nodded and agreed on this point at least. He

let the captain go about his business and came to join me once more.

'You are heartless,' I hissed, still feeling the smart of the convict's stare. I heard the bang of the hatches and the sliding of metal bolts.

''Tis true, my head rules my heart on every occasion,' he retorted, taking care to stand to one side as the redcoats left the ship. 'It is well that you know that, Annie, so you may forget any attempt to seek out a softness in my nature, which is not there and never has been, I swear to God!'

I recalled then his cold parting from the woman I took for his mother. 'We sail across the ocean for forty days and nights,' I muttered, dreading the voyage yet hoping that there might thereafter be an end to my suffering at Butler's hands.

He nodded, leaning over the broad rail to watch men on the wharf unhitch the ship's ropes from its moorings. 'And then freedom,' he said quietly, snatching a glance at me to detect what I might be thinking.

'Freedom!' I repeated. I felt the rain trickle down my cold cheeks, turned and quickly went down to my cabin.

We supped that night at the captain's table, alone among the passengers who had paid for their passage.

I found, as before, that Captain Andrews had taken

a liking to me, overcoming his natural reserve and trying to coax me out of my shyness, as he thought it. He told me fondly of his own daughter, who lived with her mother in Virginia.

'Her name is Jenny and she is ten years old,' he confided while Butler was busy with his roasted leg of lamb. 'She is fair like her mother and her hair curls to her waist. Her eyes are deepest blue.'

'And shall you see her when we reach America?' I asked.

'God willing,' the captain answered. 'Now, Annie, you know that there are other girls aboard to keep you company?'

Looking around the room where we dined, I picked out two small girls among the group of some thirty passengers from the great cabin. Beside them sat two boys under my own age, and one larger than me, but not older than fourteen or fifteen.

'That is the Miller family,' Captain Andrews explained. 'The father is a farmer eager to grow maize and tobacco in the New World, having tired of farming sheep in the north country. The mother is a seamstress, and though they are poor people, the children may provide you with some amusement.'

'Annie will keep to herself,' Butler broke in, dashing any hopes of friendship with any of our fellow passengers. 'She will not keep company with poor farmers!'

I blushed and looked down at my food which I had scarcely touched.

'Let us wait and see,' Andrews murmured under his breath. 'Customs change when we are far out to sea. In a fierce storm, a beggar may talk with a king!'

'You are not to indulge in idle chatter!' Butler insisted early the next morning, as the great ship eased its way down the wide river. We stood on the deck watching the houses slide by, leaving behind the great city and heading eastwards down the estuary.

Below deck I could hear the cries and groans of the convicts, almost drowned by the creak of timbers and flap of sails in the wind.

'Stand to one side!' came a cry, and we looked to see Dick Trapp sliding back the bolts on the iron hatch and heaving open the doors.

The cries of the shackled men grew louder.

'Stand aside!' he shouted into the hold, then pitched four loaves of dry bread into the foul darkness. A stone bottle containing water followed, lowered on a rope.

Shocked, I backed away against the rail, only to bump into Mrs Miller, the poor farmer's wife, carrying the smallest of her babies and watching the land slip away behind us. I turned and saw that she had tears in her eyes and that her face was weary and worn.

'Make room, woman!' Butler snapped, pushing her away and pulling me back towards him.

Out of the corner of my eye I saw the husband step forward as if to argue with my father for his rudeness, but his wife prevented him.

'No gossip,' Butler reminded me. 'Let them think you are a lady and far above them!'

I set my face in a frown and hurried away. It was to be a long and dreary forty days, it seemed, but freedom held out its arms and welcomed me, and so I thought I could submit to live in silence until we reached Virginia.

On Monday afternoon the captain cast anchor at Bugby's Hole and sent a boat ashore to collect gin, brandy and rum for the voyage, together with fruit such as lemons and oranges. To my surprise, Butler went ashore with the boat, leaving me in the captain's charge.

The day was fair, the sun almost warm, and so Andrews ordered the hatches to be opened to give the convicts air.

'What business does your father have on shore?' he asked me as I stood beside him on the quarterdeck, glad of the breeze running through my hair.

I had taken Butler's warning to heart and said I did not know, though I suspected he had gone to order more clothes to be delivered tomorrow or the next day when the ship anchored in Gravesend.

'You are quieter than my Jenny,' Captain Andrews

remarked, studying me for a while. 'She is full of chatter and laughter. You are very grave.'

Then he must have remembered the recent death of my mother and smiled kindly at me and said he hoped the sea air would revive my spirits.

He took me down to the main deck then and left me while he went about his business.

I walked the deck until I was interrupted by the Miller boy who was the oldest of the family of five children.

'My name is Jack Miller,' he said, facing me boldly and standing in my way. 'What is yours?'

'I am . . . Annie Butler,' I replied, eyeing him warily to see if he had noticed my hesitation. He was tall, with an unremarkable face and cropped brown hair.

'Your father keeps you close by him,' the boy observed, looking to see if Butler was nearby.

'He says I should not talk with the other passengers,' I replied stiffly.

'Too much the lady!' Jack laughed, as though my rank amused him. 'My father says we sail to the New World to free ourselves of lords and ladies. There we may own land and grow fat on it without a landlord to oppress us.'

'I wish you luck,' I said, turning away, only to find Jack's two small brothers in my path. They looked up at me with large, dark eyes and I could not help smiling at their sweet faces.

'I'm Christopher,' the largest one said, holding out his hand to me.

'Richard,' the little boy lisped.

I solemnly shook them both by the hand. 'I am Annie Butler,' I replied, more confidently this time.

The little boys nodded. Hand in hand they followed me across the deck and down to my cabin, where they came in and climbed on to the bed, sitting with their legs dangling, staring happily at me.

And so I had made friends without meaning to, and I found comfort in the sweet innocence of the children's smiles.

Our ship the *Good Endeavour* waited one day at Bugby and three days at Gravesend, as Captain Andrews had said, bringing on further provisions and waiting for tides and fair weather.

Already the sturdy frigate had become my home. I felt comfortable with the water lapping against the ship's sides as I lay in my cabin, and breathed deep the fresh air on deck. Captain Andrews continued to be kind to me, admiring the new clothes which Butler had recently brought on board.

'Yellow becomes you,' he told me on the Thursday evening as we sat at his table to dine. 'It brings out your dark colouring.'

As always, I blushed and found no reply, glancing

down at my fine yellow silk bodice and skirt of deep orange.

'The captain admires you,' Butler said. 'You must thank the gentleman, Annie!'

This made my face redden the more, as the company laughed and I caught the curious eye of Jack Miller, sitting at a long table below.

Luckily Captain Andrews smoothed over my blushes and called for the boatswain, Bill Carthy, to sing a song for us and keep us entertained.

'What song would you have?' Bill asked, standing close to me, his hands clasped behind his back, a ready smile playing across his face.

'A song of the sea,' Butler demanded, his eye on me as if warning me to stay quiet now and not to admit that I knew anything of the common songs sung by sailors in the inns around the country.

'Let it be "The Royal Oak",' Andrews decided.

Bill cleared his throat and began.

> *'As we was sailing all on the salt seas,*
> *We hadn't sailed months past but two or three,*
> *Not before we saw ten sail of Turks,*
> *All men-o'-war full as big as we.'*

It was a song I had heard many times, and one I had sung myself at my father's request, so without thought I grew ready to join in the refrain.

'Pull down your colours, you English dogs!
Pull down your colours, do not refuse.'

I mouthed the words softly until I caught Butler's angry gaze, then I remembered myself and fell silent.

'Oh pull down your colours, you English dogs,
Or else your precious life you'll lose!'

Bill Carthy's voice was lively and pure, the song lilting along. Soon many listeners had joined in, tapping their feet and raising their voices.

'Our captain being a valiant man,
And a well bespoken young man were he:
"Oh, it never shall be said that we died like dogs,
But we will fight them most manfully!"'

I sat now without a smile on my face, fearing to give myself away, glad when the song finished and the company broke up.

'Stay and drink, Mister Butler!' the captain cried as my false father got up to go to his cabin. 'Tomorrow we leave England's shores. It is time for a toast with good brandy wine!'

I saw Butler pause and fall to temptation at mention of the brandy, for he had always been a drinking man and would not stop now. And so I was able to steal away to my cabin alone, passing by the long table where my young friends, the Millers, sat. The little boys cried out my name, while the weary mother holding the baby hushed them. The father and a girl aged about nine watched me without speaking.

'Come and sit with us!' a voice cried, and I saw that Jack Miller had stood up to block my way. 'Come, Annie, you cannot ignore us for a month or more while we are at sea!'

I planned at first to sweep by, but feared this would bring more notice to me, and so stopped to speak with them. I shook hands with the father, Matthew Miller, and his wife, Alice, who told me the baby's name was Hannah and the grown girl who sat by the father was called Maggie.

I paled at this and had to hide my reaction. Indeed, a closer look told me that this Maggie looked much as I had done at nine years of age. She had the same glossy, dark curls and thin face, though her eyes were grey and mine were brown.

'Sit, Annie,' Mr Miller invited me. He had a deep, even voice and an easy manner. 'None of us will bite!'

I sat then, hoping that Butler, whose back was turned, would not notice.

'What takes you and your father to the New World?' the farmer asked in a friendly manner.

'The same thing as you, I suppose,' I replied uneasily. 'We wish to buy land and grow crops.'

Jack's father smiled. 'I did not take your father for a tiller of the soil!' he joked. 'His hands do not have the look of a plain farmer!'

'It is a new venture,' I explained, anxious to leave the table before more questions were thrown at me. I got up then and said my goodnights, only to find Jack following me.

'I can make my own way to my cabin,' I told him firmly.

But he would not be shaken off. Instead, he opened doors for me and followed close on my heels. 'What really takes you to America?' he quizzed.

'I have told you already,' I retorted.

'It is a long journey to make for your father to plant potatoes and beans,' he laughed. 'Come, Annie, you must have family in Virginia, and a large estate to go to.'

I sighed then and came out with Butler's lie about my dead mother, which did the trick and stopped Jack in his tracks.

His face turned serious and his light hazel eyes took on a look of sadness. 'That's hard,' he murmured. 'I am sorry for you.'

I shook my head and tried to pass by him in the narrow passage. 'Please ask me no more questions.'

'No, I am truly sorry, Annie.' Quietly Jack stepped to one side. 'Only, you are so very secretive.'

Once more I shook my head. 'Ask no questions and

be told no lies!' I flashed back at him, shaken by the intense look he gave me. And now I saw that his face was not unremarkable as I had at first thought, but well shaped, with eyes that bore strange flecks of colour – golden brown and green mixed together.

'Lies?' he echoed, his look turning to puzzlement.

'No. Forget what I have said. Leave me alone!' I rushed past him, my thoughts scattered, only fearing that I had said too much.

I felt Jack Miller's bright eyes still on me as I opened and shut my cabin door and flung myself down upon my bed.

Four

You cannot imagine my feelings when the *Endeavour* left Gravesend and set sail at last for the New World.

My heart was squeezed within my chest. My eyes hungered for a last view of the land that I knew.

'Do not look back,' Bill Carthy advised. He saw that I was the last of the passengers on the deck, staring into the far distance behind me. 'Look ahead.'

At what? My future was empty, impossible to foretell.

I turned seaward and saw only grey waves and low clouds driven by the wind. Gulls flew overhead, screeching at us then dropping out of sight. Hope plummeted with them and sank beneath the water.

We were off the western coast of Ireland when our first storm hit.

The captain saw it roll towards us from the south-west and readied the ship, so that when the sky darkened overhead and the giant waves struck, our sails were furled and the hatches made tight.

I was below deck in my cabin. It was past midnight and all was dark.

The swelling sea tossed us first this way and then that, and now the water did not lap gently at our sides, but smashed against us, sending shudders from bow to stern. The timbers of the ship creaked and groaned loudly.

I endured the sickening movement for what seemed like many hours. Sometimes I was thrown from my bed and fell upon the floor. At others I clung tight as the ship tossed and rolled. In the darkness, my head filled with thoughts of drowning.

At last I could bear the lonely fears no more, and wrapping my cloak around me, I wrenched open the door of my cabin. There were no lights in the passage, only the sound of the waves surging over the deck above my head. Should I go on? What would I find if I went up on deck?

A sudden roll of the ship thrust me forward towards the stairs, which I quickly clambered up, like a man buried alive and desperate to claw his way out of the grave. I came out into the air to find the deck awash and sailors running hither and thither.

'The wind drives us onshore!' the ship's mate yelled from his lookout on the ship's prow. A flash of lightning lit up the rocky coast where the white waves crashed and foamed.

Captain Andrews called commands from the

quarterdeck. Ropes uncoiled about my feet and snaked across the deck, sails were unfurled. I heard them flap into life and saw them belly out above my head.

'Go below, Annie!' Bill Carthy cried as the wind caught him and sent him staggering against the rail.

Still the salt waves swept the deck, covering the hatches and flooding into the hold.

Down below, the wretched prisoners roared in fearful desperation. 'Will you leave us to drown like rats? Have pity, for Heaven's sake!'

Still the *Endeavour* sailed nearer to the jagged rocks. Other passengers now staggered on deck, including Matthew and Jack Miller, together with Butler, just roused from his sleep. I clung to a rail beneath the captain's quarterdeck, filled with a dreadful certainty that we would soon be shipwrecked and die a watery death.

But our captain was a skilful navigator and for an hour or more he fought the wind to keep us clear of the shore. In the darkness, the convicts' cries grew more desperate still.

Captain Andrews at last felt pity for the men. 'Unchain them and bring them on deck!' he ordered, sending Trapp with his keys into the hold.

The mate swore and complained under his breath, but went and drew back the bolts. He disappeared into the foul hole and reappeared minutes later at the head of the line of prisoners, still chained together at the wrists but now unshackled at their feet so that they might climb the ladder out of the hold. They emerged shivering and dripping, escaping from drowning but frightened anew by the looming rocks.

'Andrews should leave them to their fate,' Butler muttered, sheltering like me under the overhanging quarterdeck.

A flash of lightning lit the ragged creatures as they staggered towards the rail.

I am dead and have gone to hell! was the notion that now filled my mind.

A sailor half ran, half slid across the deck, dragging a thick rope behind him. A loose barrel rolled by, crashing into the wooden pillar which supported the quarterdeck. Still the fingers of black rock beckoned.

And then a mighty wave struck the ship, tilting us to the port side, flinging every soul across the deck until we wedged together against the rail before the ship righted herself and the captain steered us round a headland towards a wide bay which I saw beneath the rail in the grey light of early dawn.

The bay opened up before us, offering calmer waters and a gentle slope of white sand instead of the treacherous rocks behind.

I closed my eyes in disbelief. When I opened them again, I started back from the face of one of the convicts. His stinking breath was upon me, his eyes wild and rolling in his head.

It was Jack Miller who pulled me clear from beneath this wretch, pushing him away and standing me back on my feet. The ship was steadier now, the wind and rain less fierce.

'A puff of wind blows you over!' he grinned. 'You are light as a feather, Annie Butler!'

'We are within a hair's breadth of drowning, every one of us!' I exclaimed. 'And yet you find time to tease me and make fun!'

Around us, sailors and fellow passengers righted themselves and Trapp brought the chained men together by the gaping hold.

However, one of the convicts cursed more than the others, complaining that his arm was broken in the violent storm and they must unchain him, for he was in great pain.

Reluctantly, the ship's mate conferred with the captain, who said he must first loosen the chain and then send the ship's doctor to attend the man.

'Let him rot!' Butler said again as Trapp followed his order. This time my father's comment was loud enough for the man to hear.

And then the freed convict rounded on us, flinging himself at my false father, broken arm or no. The two fell to the deck, into a shadowy corner, wrestling and rolling, kicking with their feet, until Butler at last managed to land a blow against the convict's chin.

The man fell back limply and Butler stood up. His

lip was bleeding, his hat blowing free across the deck.

The injured man stared up in the half-light. I saw an alteration in his face – a look perhaps of surprised recognition – before Trapp fell upon him and dragged him away.

Then the doctor came, drunk from the liquor he had downed during the storm to quell his fears.

The captain saw this from his deck and ordered the man back below. 'How do you fare, sir?' he asked Butler, who had retrieved his hat.

Butler too had caught the convict's startled look and was unnerved. 'I would have the villain horsewhipped!' he cried, wiping the blood from his mouth. 'I warned you, Captain, that I did not like the prospect of sharing my passage with convicted men!'

'And I do not like passengers brawling aboard my ship, whether they be gentlemen or prisoners,' Andrews replied, ordering Trapp to tend to the convict's injuries, which he did roughly enough.

The man groaned and cursed, swearing to God that Butler was no gentleman, as all on board would soon find out. 'Imposter!' he muttered under his breath. 'If I am not mistaken, you have a date with the hangman in York!'

Enraged once more, Butler drew the pistol concealed beneath his coat, which I knew he always carried with him since our escape from York. He took unsteady aim at the man.

For a moment everyone on deck stood still. Then Trapp let the convict go, leaving him to his fate. Butler's aim steadied. He had his enemy in his sights. But in a flash, before Butler could pull the trigger, Jack Miller and his father threw themselves upon him, knocking him to the ground. The shot went off into the air. None were harmed.

'Mister Butler, give me your gun and go to your cabin!' Captain Andrews cried, striding down from the quarterdeck.

Forced to comply, Butler slunk away. Then the captain dealt harshly with the convict, telling him that he would not be allowed on deck again during the whole voyage. 'You are to blame!' he insisted as the man muttered and swore. 'You are a convicted man and must expect rude treatment from your fellow passengers who are decent, law-abiding men who pay an honest way towards a new life!'

The convict spat on the deck. 'There's what I think of your decent, law-abiding man!' he cried.

I shook and trembled, every second fearing revelation.

But Trapp overpowered the convict before he could say more, making him cry out in pain as he dragged him towards the prisoners' hold. Soon he was safely below deck and our ship sailed into the calm waters of Galway Bay.

Five

Fear forced me back into the web of Butler's lies.

The sailors repaired the damage done by the storm, running about the ship with hammer and nails, sewing tears in the sails, packing oakum into the hull to make it watertight once more. Meanwhile my father kept to his cabin, and me with him.

'The villain knows me!' he swore in a low voice. 'You heard what he said to me beneath his breath!'

'What shall we do?' I whispered.

'He knows me and intends to ruin me!' Butler continued. 'But I am prepared.'

'If they discover the truth, will they take us from the ship and send us back to England?'

'Be quiet and listen!' Butler snapped, sitting me down in the chair. 'We will be ready for him and we will deny everything. Especially you, Annie. Think hard. Who will they believe – a common thief or an innocent girl?'

'I will deny it,' I echoed faintly, seeing no other way.

'And in case he will not be silenced we must find out who this man is and how he knows my history.' Butler thought ahead, opening up the sea chest which he kept in the corner of his cabin and unlocking the secret drawer. 'Then we must buy his secrecy.'

'And if he will not be bought?' I asked. Fear had weakened me. I sat in terror of discovery.

'All men may be bought,' Butler sneered, taking out a small purse of gold coins. He slipped three golden guineas and some lesser coins into his deep coat pocket, restored the purse to its secret place then locked the chest. 'I will begin with Mister Trapp, the first mate!'

Dick Trapp was a man whom none liked but everyone feared. Nearing fifty years of age, but still strong as an ox, his face was always frowning, his voice angry. No sailor crossed him, no passenger ever conversed with him.

In short, I thought he was a man who needed nothing and no one, whom money could not buy. But I was an innocent abroad, as you shall see.

With the weather set fair and the *Endeavour* shipshape once more, we sailed out of Galway Bay into the wide ocean, encountering no obstacle for three days or more.

And so I settled into the habits of a seafarer. I rose at dawn to stroll the deck before breakfast, gazed at the flat horizon, idled away my days in reading or sewing, always afraid of the violent man in the prisoners' hold below my feet.

Butler meanwhile was busy with his plan.

'Mister Trapp,' says he, accosting the first mate during our first day out of Galway Bay. 'Will you eat and drink with me tonight?'

Trapp looked sideways at him. 'I take my meat with the men, sir,' he muttered in a surly voice.

'But for once, join me,' Butler urged, turning on the charm. 'I wish to say thank you for restraining the villain who threw himself at me.'

'I wanted no blood spilt on the deck,' Trapp said, abruptly turning away until Butler sidestepped and came around to the front of him again.

'You are not a soft-hearted man, Mister Trapp.'

The mate shook his head and grunted.

'Then we are alike,' Butler said coolly. 'You do not care much for the convicts in your charge?'

'They mean nothing to me,' Trapp agreed. I could see he grew interested in Butler's reasons for engaging him in conversation, and more curious still when Butler drew a coin from his pocket.

'I need the name of the man who attacked me,' Butler said in a low voice, holding up the half guinea piece.

Trapp tilted his head to one side and stared at the money.

Butler drew out another half guinea. 'The name and the crime for which he was transported!'

Trapp took the first coin between his big thumb and forefinger. 'Robert Unthank, one-time blacksmith of Wetherby.' He paused until Butler placed the other coin in his open palm. 'Convicted of house burglary in the York assizes, held for four weeks in the gaol there, awaiting transportation.'

Butler nodded.

Both men turned away. It was as if they had never spoken. Trapp did not come to dine with us that evening.

'That is how he knows me!' Butler was now convinced that Unthank posed a major danger to us in our attempt to start a new life. 'He was in the gaol when we were brought there. Every day that passes aboard this ship, he has the power to destroy us!'

He paced the deck early on the fifth day of our voyage, with me at his side. There was a terrible restlessness about him, as if he had not slept.

'You hoped they would not believe him,' I reminded him. 'The man has no proof that we are not who we say we are.'

'Yet he may use the truth as a weapon,' he insisted. 'There is a rabble below deck who know my name and reputation. Some would willingly betray me.'

And so Butler's fame as the smuggler Tom Hague

played against him and I was once more in the shadow of the hangman's noose.

'I can hardly pay all thirteen to keep my secret,' Butler said, glancing up at the quarterdeck. 'And since the night of the storm, our good captain watches me with the eyes of a hawk!'

This was true. I had noticed that Captain Andrews had cooled towards Butler, though he was still kind to me.

'How long will Unthank wait before he unmasks me?' Butler wondered, striding impatiently from port to starboard. 'How much must I pay him for his silence?'

I had no answer to these questions, but lived on a knife-edge, like my tormentor.

We were seven days out to sea and Butler had taken to drinking hard when I fell in again with Jack Miller. I was sewing on deck, sitting in a warm midday breeze. Butler was below with his brandy and lemon, which had become an increasing habit with him.

'Annie, you are avoiding us since we saved the convict from your father's pistol!' he called from the prow of the ship where he used a knife to whittle a shape on to a thick piece of wood. He came closer to where I sat with my stitching. 'I see you are no seamstress,' he laughed.

I frowned as I looked up. 'And I see you are no carver of wood!' I replied.

He held up the crude shape of a doll's head and body. 'For Maggie,' he explained. 'My mother is teaching her to sew clothes for the puppet.'

I nodded, thought much but said nothing.

Jack sat beside me. 'Are you contented, Annie?'

The question surprised me. I held my silence.

'You do not look content,' he continued, scraping at the wood with his knife. 'There is something about you that says you are afraid.'

'Of what? Of whom?' I shot back, catching my finger with the point of the needle and giving a small gasp.

Jack paused a long while, watching me suck my sore finger. 'Of your father,' he said quietly, getting up then and walking away, leaving me in confusion.

The Atlantic Ocean held us in her bosom, rocking us gently, giving us a fair wind for Virginia.

Butler brooded and drank so heavily that the captain no longer invited him to his table to dine. Often he kept to his cabin, planning how to outwit Unthank, either by bribery or cruel violence against his enemy.

This gave me time to myself and the freedom to walk or work on deck, where I became a common sight at certain parts of the day. Bill Carthy in particular liked to greet me as he went about his work, humming a tune and grinning at me whenever he passed by.

'*As I sailed out one day, one day,*' he sang, '*And being not far from land, And there I spied a mermaid sitting on a rock . . .*'

'*. . . With a comb and a glass in her hand.*' I sang soft and low, carried along by the rhythm and unable to prevent myself.

Bill smiled and nodded. 'Ah, little Annie, you know the song of "The Mermaid"!'

I shook my head hard.

'Yes, and you have the sweetest voice,' he insisted. He called Jack Miller across. 'Annie sings like a bird!' he proclaimed. 'Sing something for Jack, Annie, my dove!'

I refused of course, but though Bill went on his way, Jack sat beside me.

'Secretive as ever,' he chided. 'Well, if you will not sing for me, I suppose I must recount my own history to fill in the many hours and days we must spend in each other's company.'

'Why must you?' I retorted, keeping a wary eye open for my father.

'Merely to be friendly,' Jack explained. 'And because I don't want to pry into things you do not wish to tell me.'

'Very well,' I agreed. 'What was your home in England?'

'We lived in the north of the country, nestled among the hills. My father tended a flock of sheep for one of the great landowners there, whose name I will not share with you because I cannot speak well of him yet would not blacken his character without the man here to defend himself.'

'You are very fair,' I commented, keeping my head bowed over the piece of needlework I had resumed when Bill Carthy had thrown us together.

'My father taught me to speak plain and true,' Jack said. 'Indeed, it was through plain speaking that he fell out with our cruel landlord, who was so high and mighty that he thought all must bow before his wishes even when they caused great harm.'

'Tell me what you mean,' I said, relieved to have the attention taken away from me.

'There was a poor family in our neighbourhood who grazed their cattle on common land. But the landowner laid false claim to this small patch of land and turned the family away in the middle of harsh winter, so that they would have starved if my father had not given them shelter.

'Then my father went to the great house and argued that the land did not belong to the estate, which angered the great man more, and he turned us out of our home in the week before Christmas – my mother and father, and all five children, with the baby just born.'

I shook my head in dismay.

'Now we are poor but free,' Jack went on. 'Father and I work to feed the family, while Mother takes in sewing. We have set our hopes on the New World, and God willing we will do well.'

I could not hide my admiration as Jack concluded his story, and I envied the future that lay before him. 'I would give much for a family like yours,' I sighed, glad when Maggie and the small boy, Richard, appeared on deck and came towards us.

Richard held out his arms and I lifted him on to my knee. 'Sing me a song!' he begged, clutching at me with his chubby fingers.

I looked at Maggie then, who clutched the doll Jack had made for her. She told us shyly that Mister Carthy had said that I had a fine voice.

'Then he was wrong to do so,' I argued, melting however under the little boy's pleas. After all, what harm could it do? 'Very well, I will sing you the song of Geordie.'

Holding the fair-haired boy on my knee, I began softly at first.

> *'As I came over London Bridge*
> *One misty morning early,*
> *I overheard a fair pretty maid*
> *Lamenting for her Geordie.'*

Richard put his arms around my neck and we swayed together. Maggie and Jack sat quietly at my side.

> ' "Come bridle me my milk-white horse,
> Come bridle me my pony,
> That I may ride to London's court,
> To plead for the life of Geordie." '

I sang louder now, and my voice rose above the sound of the gentle waves into the open blue sky. I did not notice other passengers gather, leaning back my head and singing the lament of the maid pleading for the life of the man she loved.

> 'The judge looked over his left shoulder,
> And said, "I'm sorry for thee.
> My pretty fair maid, you come too late,
> For he's condemned already." '

The song ended sadly, as most old songs do, and left my audience in silence, until Richard begged to know why Geordie must die.

'Because he stole the King's deer,' Maggie told him, handing him her doll and lifting him from my knee.

'Bill Carthy was right – you sing like a bird,' Jack said brightly. 'Like a bird freed from its cage and soaring into the sky!'

'A nightingale!' Matthew Miller said, standing to the rear of the group, head and shoulders above the other spectators.

I smiled then, and the truth was on my lips. 'My

name is Maggie Nightingale!' I wanted to declare. But of course it was the old fear and dread of the hangman's noose that prevented me.

'I will have Unthank killed and that will stop his mouth for good!' Butler decided at last, after many days spent brooding over the problem. 'One of the convicts in that hell-hole will do the job for me!'

'But others will know our secret,' I reminded him, thinking that if Butler put an end to Unthank's life, he must take the lives of twelve other convicts too. 'Do you imagine that he has kept silent after what happened during the storm?'

Butler waved aside the argument. 'One will be enough,' he insisted. 'It will be a warning to the others, who will not dare speak out.'

I remembered then how Tom Hague had ruled by fear in the fishing towns of the north-east coast, setting spies amongst us, threatening violence to any who had stood in his way. And so another murder was to be committed in cold blood, and I must stand by in silence.

'My only problem will be to get to the man who will do the deed.' Butler thought aloud, leaning over the deck rail to gaze down at the white wave trailing in the wake of our sturdy ship. 'It is true that the prisoners are brought up on deck when the captain wishes, is it not?'

I nodded, knowing that Captain Andrews had given

the chained men more liberty since we had sailed out into the wide sea. Each day towards the end of the afternoon, he gave the order to Trapp to have the men parade on deck to breathe the fresh air – all save Unthank, who stayed below. But I took care to be out of sight on these occasions, not wanting to see how the convicts suffered, nor for them to set eyes on me.

'Good,' Butler said, his grey eyes hooded, his expression sly. 'Tomorrow!' he added, pulling down the brim of his hat.

Six

It is a mark of the man's cunning that I had no notion of how Butler would carry out his new plan.

I only knew that when I woke up next day there was a change in his manner, which had grown more brisk. I noticed too that he put aside his stone bottle of brandy and that he did not sit and brood inside his cabin.

'Good morning, Captain!' he called up to the quarterdeck. 'Is the wind behind us? Are we still set fair?'

Andrews replied that our progress was good, though there was a storm ahead, driving in from the north-west.

'Will it hit us as hard as the last one?' Butler inquired.

'I hope to steer the ship safely to the south,' came the brief reply.

Butler walked the deck with me then, greeting fellow passengers, though he turned away from Matthew and Alice Miller with a scowl. 'God spare me from honest men!' he muttered scornfully, bringing me to a halt beside the bolted hatch that covered the convicts' hold.

Is he mad? I wondered, thinking that he intended to crouch down by the grille to make his deadly bargain.

But he merely stared down between the bars into the foul darkness, listening to the rattle of chains and the low groans of the men. 'A golden guinea will be enough!' he declared. 'And tonight I will sleep easy in my bed.'

The afternoon came, and with it the time for the convicts to be brought on deck. Butler insisted on us taking the air once more, though we were the only passengers to brave the strengthening wind, the others having kept below deck.

'Have a care how you walk, Mister Butler!' Bill Carthy called from a spot high in the rigging, where he tightened knots and checked the sails. 'Keep to the leeward side!'

We walked out of sight, under the overhang of the quarterdeck where we waited until Butler spotted Trapp carrying a large set of keys. The first mate unlocked and then unbolted the hatch then ordered the chained men to climb up on deck.

I pressed myself back, as far out of view as I could, dreading the sight of the convicts.

Butler glanced down at me. 'Still too soft-hearted,

Annie! Your pity does them no good and only makes you wretched. You must try to curb it.'

Still I puzzled over which prisoner he had chosen to commit the crime and how he meant to draw near and talk with the man. I soon found out, however.

'Say nothing!' he warned, suddenly seizing me by the arm and thrusting me down into a dark space where kegs of rum and brandy were stored.

Gasping, I stared up at him.

'When the sailors come upon you, say you fell down amongst the barrels and fainted away!' Without waiting for a reply, he turned and with a cry of alarm ran towards the first mate and his prisoners.

'Trapp, you must help me!' he shouted. 'It is my daughter, Annie. I cannot find her, though I have searched the deck from prow to stern!'

I heard Trapp growl his reply, then my father spoke again.

'Help me, man! Run to the prow, seek her there! I fear she has been caught by the wind and fallen overboard!'

Lying villain! I thought to myself, crouching between the barrels, realising that I was well and truly caught in Butler's snare once more.

What could Trapp do but follow my distressed 'father's' earnest request? I heard heavy footsteps run towards the prow of the ship and pictured Butler striding in amongst the convicts, choosing one, showing him a shiny guinea and quickly explaining under his breath what he would have him do to earn it.

The footsteps returned. 'Your daughter is not there,' Trapp reported. 'Carthy is up in the rigging. He says he saw you walking with her not five minutes since.'

'That is true,' Butler confirmed, pretending to run hither and thither, drawing other sailors into the search. 'My poor girl! If she is lost, I am all alone in this world!'

I waited with a sickness in my heart. At last, one of the sailors thought to search below deck and they soon came upon me, trapped among the kegs of spirits.

'She is here. She is not drowned!' he called, lifting me up from the floor and hoisting me back on deck, while other men came running.

Butler was first among them. He took me in his arms and I made sure to look as though I was faint, as he had told me. 'Annie, my girl!' he cried, grasping me to him and striding across the deck. 'How did you come to fall down there?'

I wished for all the world that he had not forced me to lie out loud for him and make me part of his evil deception. But his cold eyes glared secretly at me, and answer I must. 'The wind caught me and blew me,' I stammered, hiding my shamed face against his chest. 'I must have fallen into a swoon.'

'Nicely said!' he muttered, turning to face Trapp and his men.

I saw the convicts in the distance, huddled miserably together, staring at Butler and me. 'I am sick!' I sighed, turning my face away.

So my false father carried me to my cabin and straightaway stood me on my feet with a look of triumph. 'Nicely spoken!' he said again, standing back with his legs wide apart, his hands on his hips. He laughed and said, 'The plan is laid. I warrant the villain would have done the deed for *half* a guinea!'

'Truly, I am sick in my stomach!' I wept, trembling all over at the thought of what I had helped to set in motion.

'And I will sleep tonight!' he said heartily. 'For that traitor Unthank will never see the light of dawn!'

Nightmares crowded on me thick and fast. I saw again the skeleton walking in the fog in St Mary's churchyard, heard again the blast of cannons firing at us from the high cliff. Then I was on a ship in a storm, heading for jagged rocks, then back in Saltersgate under a hail of soldier's bullets. Again I saw my poor father's face as it was when he was alive, beseeching us to come in through the door, then again when he was dead and all the blood had drained from his dear face.

I woke and sat bolt upright. The windowless cabin felt like my own coffin.

I could sleep no more.

* * *

It was true, I was sick. A fever seized me that night and by morning, when a knock came at my door, a cold sweat covered me and my bones ached.

The knock came again, louder this time.

'I am not well. I have a fever!' I called out, thinking that the dreadful deed was done and Butler had come to gloat.

'Annie, it is Jack Miller. Bill Carthy tells me you were almost lost at sea!'

'Go away, Jack!' I pleaded.

But the cabin door opened and he took a step inside. 'I want to see for myself that you are not a ghost come back to haunt us!'

'I did not drown,' I insisted, through chattering teeth. 'But I have a fever, as you see. Besides, if my father finds you here, he will throw *you* overboard and there will be an end!'

'Let him try,' Jack muttered, seeing that I was pale and cold. 'Do you have water to drink?'

Shaking my head, I struggled to put my feet on the ground. I let Jack wrap a blanket around my shoulders. 'I am wretched,' I cried in my weakness. 'Oh Jack, you do not know what I have done!'

'It cannot be anything very bad,' he said kindly, but growing uncomfortable at my tears.

I looked up at him. 'You do not know me, else you would not be so kind.'

'I know that you are ill with a fever and that my

mother has herbs that will purge it,' he replied. 'I will fetch her this instant.'

I could not let him go without first asking what I dreaded to hear. 'Jack, is there fresh news aboard ship this morning?'

He shook his head. 'No news but the old news.'

'. . . Is Trapp on deck?'

'He is,' Jack replied, growing puzzled at my agitation. 'He stands in the prow with his telescope, studying the horizon. Why do you ask?'

'Do you know – has he fed the prisoners? Is there trouble in the hold?'

'Annie, you are not well. Let me fetch my mother!'

'Wait. You are sure there is no news?'

'None!' Jack declared, making me lie down and promising that he would soon return. 'Whatever you fear has not happened. Rest now and try to be calm.'

And so for a few minutes more I clung to the hope that Butler's plan had failed and that no violent death had occurred on board the *Good Endeavour*.

Jack soon returned with his mother, who brought with her a preparation of herbs to draw my fever out. The liquid was warm and bitter to the taste, but I accepted the kindness, wondering why it was that the sound of voices had not woken Butler in his cabin next door.

'How bad is she?' Jack asked his mother, who plumped my pillows and made me lie on my bed.

'She will do well enough when she has rested,' the good woman replied. 'But she seems uneasy in her mind.'

'Aye and she will not say what troubles her,' he frowned. 'She holds her secret like a limpet clinging to a rock!'

Alice stroked my feverish brow. 'What is it, child?' she murmured.

And in my agony I might have told them all, except that Butler did wake at last and staggered from his cabin, his head still clouded from strong spirits, his features slack from sleep. He saw Jack and his mother and straight away roared foul oaths at them, threatening that he would smash the boy's skull if he came near his daughter.

Jack would have retorted, but his mother pulled him back and hurried him away, leaving me to face my father alone.

Butler came close and hung over me, pushing his face close to mine. 'If you breathe a word of our situation, I will kill you!' he snarled. 'I will snap you like a twig under my feet, and with no more thought for the consequences!'

I shuddered and protested that I had not betrayed him. 'I am sick with a fever!' I protested as he pulled me upright.

'Put on your cloak,' Butler insisted, slowly coming to his senses and taking his watch from his pocket. 'Let us see what news the day brings.'

Though weak, I struggled to do as he said, following him along the corridor and up on deck, where the cool morning air cut through my weakened frame.

Butler took my arm and made me walk with him. 'Take care, Annie,' he warned, seeing Alice Miller with her husband. 'If they ask, say you are well.' He steered me away from the other passengers, towards the hold where the prisoners were kept, where he greeted the ship's mate. 'Is all well below?' he queried, as Trapp emerged from the dark hold.

Trapp rubbed his hands down the sides of his legs, as if wiping away dirt. 'Well enough for all except one,' he reported calmly. 'There is a man down there who lies dead, and twelve others who deny all knowledge of how it came about.'

I felt Butler's hand clench into a fist under my cloak. 'How did he die?'

'Strangled by a chain until all breath was drawn from his body,' Trapp said. 'So there is one less mouth to feed, at least.'

And no word of sorrow passed his lips as he reported the murder to Captain Andrews, who ordered that the body be brought up from the hold then wrapped in sailcloth and buried at sea.

I stayed on deck with Butler, watching how the news passed quickly from person to person, seeing Jack Miller regard me with new curiosity and perhaps suspicion.

Ah! he seemed to think. *Now I know why Annie was agitated and asked what news there was on deck!*

At least, my guilty conscience made me read his glance thus.

Butler, however, was triumphant. 'We have come out from under a shadow,' he gloated. 'With Unthank dead, there is no threat hanging over us and we may look ahead untroubled!

Aye, if you can stomach murder! I thought, hanging my head, and avoiding all honest gazes.

Then came a shock that brought down even the heartless butcher who had trapped me and stolen my life from me. And this is it.

Captain Andrews wished the funeral to be held swiftly. The deck was crowded as the wrapped corpse was brought up from the hold to unusual silence from the wretches below. The captain stood at the deck rail. Six sailors carried the body to him.

I hung back as far as I could, filled with dread. Butler pushed to the front of the crowd.

There was a short prayer from the captain, and a reading from a black bible which he held open before him. Then he paid a final tribute to the man who had died. 'Every man deserves decent burial, no matter what his crime,' he said solemnly.

Some people murmured their agreement. Others looked severe and shook their heads.

'We pray that this man, Henry Boyes, will find a final resting place at the side of our Lord . . .'

I saw Butler take a step forward and then stop himself. He turned, his face twisted with fury, pushing his way through the crowd to where I stood.

'. . . that his offence will be washed from his soul . . . and he may rest in peace.'

Captain Andrews ended his prayer and his men tilted the body over the rail towards the sea.

'Boyes!' Butler hissed, seizing me by the arm and marching me away before the ceremony was over. 'What name is this? This should be Unthank, for God's sake!'

The body dropped from sight. There was a great splash, then silence.

I staggered and fell to the floor. There was a yellow light and then darkness. I remember nothing else.

Seven

I continued in a swoon for several hours, sometimes half awake, but then lapsing again into darkness without the will to prevent it.

Hearing of my illness, the captain sent the ship's doctor to attend me, and he had me carried to a new cabin where there was a small window to allow in the light and air.

Days passed, and still I did not recover.

Once I woke to see the soft, fleshy face of the doctor peering down at me over his spectacles. 'She must be made to drink clean water,' he said to someone whose face I could not make out. 'Change her linen and put a cool cloth on her brow.'

On another occasion it was Butler who sat next to my bed. 'Hear this, Annie. The dead man, Boyes – he was the villain I paid to carry out the murder. It seems he was killed out of greed, for when the other convicts heard of his new wealth, they turned upon him. The result is, Boyes died and Unthank lives, though by all accounts, my enemy's health is no better than yours.

His broken bone will not heal and he has succumbed to fever. God willing, he will not reach the shore of Virginia!'

I heard Butler's words, but thought I dreamed them, my head swam so. It was filled again with Whitby ghosts, and the voice of Mally Truefit urging me to look up and be brave.

And so I roused from my fever on what turned out to be the fifth day after the death of Boyes, to find my friend Jack Miller sitting by my side.

'You are awake,' he said simply. 'I thought you meant to sleep the whole voyage through!'

Through my dry lips I managed to ask for water, which Jack gave to me by gently raising my head and letting me take a very few sips before he put down the glass. 'The doctor said you would not recover,' he told me. 'But my mother said you were young and that your will to live was strong. She has sat four nights by your side.'

'She is kinder than I deserve,' I said weakly.

'So you say, Annie. But if that is true, then it weighs in the balance against your father, who is more cruel to you than you deserve.'

'Why? What has he done?' Gradually coming to, I saw that I was in a new place – a room with sunlight which fell across my bed and cast long shadows over Jack's even features.

'It is not what he does, but what he does not do,' he

explained. 'He has not been near you more than once since you fell ill, Annie. Instead, he keeps to his cabin and they say he drinks great jugs of brandy and broods over a wrong done to him by the prisoners in the hold.'

I sighed and turned my head towards the window.

'What wrong does he mean?' Jack asked. 'What does your father have to do with the convicted men?'

Ah, if you knew! I thought. *Then you would not speak another word to me, Jack!* I asked for more water then said I must sleep.

Jack shook his head. 'Closer than a limpet on the rocks!' he sighed. 'I see he has some hold over you that you cannot break.'

'Please!' I implored him. 'I cannot speak about these things. And you must not approach my father. Promise me!'

Fearing that I would grow agitated, Jack agreed. He smoothed my blanket and made me comfortable. 'My mother is anxious over you,' he said as he opened the door, making one last attempt. 'She says you are burdened with a secret too great to bear.'

'Which I will take to my grave,' I replied, turning my head away.

I lay in bed another week, while the *Endeavour* ploughed through the clear ocean, her motion slowly rocking me back to health. In my troubled mind, I saw her as a small cork pitched this way and that across a mighty sea, sometimes tilting violently towards the depths, then rising again to face the heavens, continuing through the night, guided by the stars.

Towards what? Was there safety at the end of the rough voyage, or was there more agony?

Hague will let me go! I told myself when the sun shone in on me. *We will land in Virginia and I will be of no more use to him. He will give me my freedom.*

Or else, when the sky was dark and the moon went behind the clouds, I saw a different picture. *He will never release me! I know this man's nature to be violent and cruel. He will kill me rather than risk letting me go!*

I awoke one night in a terror. I had dreamed that my tormentor held a knife to my throat and swore he would cut out my tongue so that I might never utter the words 'Thomas Hague'.

At my side, sewing by the light of a candle, sat Alice Miller, her baby on her lap. She calmed me and spoke kindly to me, saying that I had had a nightmare.

I lay quiet for a while, listening to the sea.

'Who is Thomas Hague?' Alice asked me, her needle flying in and out of the coarse cotton cloth she sewed. 'You spoke of him in your sleep just now.'

'No one,' I replied, my heart suddenly racing.

She did not look up. 'And who is Maggie Nightingale?'

'She is no one,' I said again. *A girl who once was me, but now is dead and gone.*

144

* * *

We sailed into our third week and I grew stronger. The doctor brought Captain Andrews to see me and said that my fever had passed.

'Should you like to return to your old cabin, Annie?' Andrews asked, sitting on the chair beside my bed. 'Or should you like to stay here?'

I hesitated.

'Your father will not mind the answer you give. He stays in his cabin and does not see much of what goes on around him,' he assured me.

'Then I will stay here,' I replied, thinking that any distance I could put between myself and Butler made me safer. Indeed, the horror I had felt after the murder of Boyes had begun to loosen its grip, and I was growing to be more my old self. I managed to smile at the captain and to thank him for his kindness.

He looked at me for a long time, his eyes searching into mine. 'There is a strange feeling on board that makes me uneasy,' he confessed. 'I have sailed this ocean many times, been through many storms and kept to my quarterdeck through wind and rain. Yet I have never felt secrets surround me as they do on this voyage.'

I bit my lip and silently begged him not to ask me questions, for this was a man who might work the truth from me.

Captain Andrews read that look and in his kindness

he sighed and stood up. 'I hope you will soon be well, child,' he said, leaving me alone again.

In the fourth week of our voyage I ventured back on deck to find Bill Carthy tending to the rigging of the ship and sailors running about their tasks as they had on our first day out to sea.

All was well, it seemed.

I sat beneath the shelter of the captain's deck, breathing the air and looking out across the waves. The shores of America lay less than a week away. Freedom beckoned.

But danger dragged me back as I felt the swell of hope within my bosom, for this was the time of day when Trapp brought the convicts on deck – eleven men who shielded their eyes against the light and rattled their chains as they walked.

I had forgotten during my illness how wretched they looked, but now that I saw them again they seemed mere skeletons. Rags hung off their starving frames, their eyes were hollow and lifeless. And whose were the hands that had strangled poor Boyes, down there in the filthy darkness? Fascinated, I studied each in turn from my quiet seat under the quarterdeck.

The men came in single file around the deck to the sound of rattling chains. Some were tall, some small, all thin and miserable. One in the middle of the procession saw me and stopped to stare, causing the one in front to strain at his chain.

'Walk on!' Trapp commanded, harsh as any gaoler.

The staring man obeyed, but his eyes followed me all the time he was on deck. And I feared what he would tell Unthank, kept chained like a dog in the hold below.

I saw Hague's girl he would say. *Large as life, playing the part of a lady when she ought to be down here with the convicted men!*

And they would talk of the pretence Hague kept up of a Lincolnshire gentleman, laughing amongst themselves because they knew Unthank had only to stand up and denounce him whenever he chose. Then our game would be up and we would be hanged.

Unthank plays a waiting game! I said to myself, shifting uneasily on the bench where I sat. I frowned as I saw my so-called father struggle up on deck – the first time I had set eyes on him since I had recovered from my fever.

He too backed off when he noticed the convicts. Then he brought himself under control, thrust back his shoulders and swaggered in front of them. They in turn muttered low, jeering comments.

'I see you have deserted me, Annie,' Butler grumbled as he reached my sheltered retreat. He was unshaven, dressed only in shirtsleeves. The wind blew strong and fresh. 'Do you prefer your new cabin so much that you would forsake my company?'

'The window gives me fresh air,' I replied, attempting to be bold, and relieved to see that Trapp was ordering the convicts back below.

Butler eyed me narrowly. 'And you keep our secret, do you?'

I nodded awkwardly.

'In three days we will be ashore. We will taste liberty.'

'And shall I be free to go?' I dared to ask, knowing however that his assurance carried less value even than the counterfeit coins he hid within his sea chest.

'Free as a bird,' he promised, staring at me with those heartless, empty eyes.

And so my fears did not ease, even though Jack Miller talked much with me during the days left on board the *Endeavour* and the small boys ran about my feet, demanding that I sing them songs.

I said I would not, until one evening, when the sun lay low on the western horizon and Maggie brought the baby Hannah to sit on my lap. Then Christopher and Richard ran up and begged me once more.

'I will sing a lullaby if you will sit by me,' I said, hoping to rock the baby to sleep. The sweet little thing stared up at me with eyes the same mixed colour as her brother Jack's.

I began by gently humming the tune in the mellow light. The boys grew content and the baby closed her eyes. Then I sang the words, drawing others to me to listen. And I forgot my troubles in the pure joy of singing, happy for that moment, until a sudden cry from the crow's nest broke the mood.

'Land ahoy!' Bill Carthy cried.

All turned towards the prow of the ship, raising their hands to shield their eyes from the low sun, longing for the first sight of land on the horizon.

'Land!' Jack Miller said, taking me by the arm and leading me to the port side. 'Our long journey is over, Annie!'

I strained to see, and at last made out a grey shape rising out of the shimmering water in the far, far distance. It was the shore of America. The New World.

Part Three

One

I could not prevent a sensation of eagerness from flowing over me when I realised that I could see America spread out before my very eyes!

The land took shape – low and hazy still, but growing more distinct as the ship drew close. We had been almost forty days at sea.

Captain Andrews shouted orders and the sailors climbed the rigging, loosening ropes ready to bring down the sails. Bill Carthy climbed down nimbly from the crow's nest and helped Trapp to prepare the rowing-boat.

Soon all the passengers were on deck, hungry for sight of Virginia. Alice Miller took her little ones forward to the prow, while Matthew and Jack set to and helped swing the small boat over the side of the ship.

I held my breath. In the golden evening light the calm sea sparkled, the land invited us. But then Butler arrived to remind me that our danger had not passed.

'Get your men to bring my sea chest up on deck!' he

yelled at Carthy, before he turned to me. 'Place your clothes into this leather satchel and put on your cloak as quick as you can. I intend to be the first off the ship, before the convicts are brought up from below.'

I saw that he was free from the effects of liquor, clean-shaven, with fresh lace at his neck and cuffs. His eyes were clear, moving restlessly across the scene on deck.

'Not so fast, Mister Butler,' Captain Andrews called down from the quarterdeck. 'My men will row into harbour this evening to find us a mooring. But you must bide your time on board ship for one more night!'

'I have no intention of waiting, Captain!' Butler took me by the arm and rushed me up the steps to talk with Andrews. The boat will take me and my daughter on to land, or I will—'

The captain did not let him proceed with his threat, but faced him squarely. 'I am captain of this ship, Mister Butler, and though, if I am frank, I would not be sorry to lose your company this very minute, still I say you shall bide your time.'

Butler clenched his jaw and muttered oaths through his teeth. 'What would be your answer if I were to pay handsomely for early passage in the boat?' he muttered, drawing a purse from his coat pocket.

Andrews' stern stare did not waver. He kept his hands clasped firmly behind his back. 'Still the same,' he replied, scarcely concealing his anger. 'Mister Butler, you must take your daughter down on deck and wait with the other passengers. The ship will sail with the tide into port at dawn tomorrow.'

We went down then and, meanwhile, the boat was lowered into the water. Three men took their place and began rowing towards the shore.

We all watched them closely as they rowed into the sunset, trying to make out the harbour and the surrounding land, able to see wooden wharves and warehouses and a flat hinterland of swamps and reeds, with dark pine forest behind. But then the light faded and night fell. Butler must submit on this occasion to another man's orders.

The hours went slowly. I lay on my bed and stared at the stars. My old life lay a world away. I was cast adrift on a huge ocean with no living soul for company except my tormentor whose true name I dared not speak. Unless . . . unless I broke from him now and made my own way, freed myself from my slave master and slid away amongst the crowd which would greet us on the wharf at daybreak . . . unless I made my own bid for freedom!

I rose before dawn and carefully packed my skirts and linen into the leather satchel. I had no money or articles of value – nothing but the clothes, which perhaps I might sell and so keep myself from starving.

If I flee, where will I go? I asked myself, going on deck and pacing to and fro. *This country is strange to me. Are there towns here where I could get employment, or will I find a farmer who will give me work? Will Butler seek me out and kill me?*

My heart began to fail me then, but I thought of what would happen if I did not escape – always living in the shadow of Butler's cruelty, his shame being my shame, with the hangman's noose above our heads, even here in the New World.

For Unthank, though ill, was still alive and able to do us harm, emerging from the convicts' hold like a grey ghost to point his finger at Thomas Hague and Maggie Nightingale, dragging us back into our past.

'I will run away!' I swore then, facing the misty land, feeling the ship rock gently under my feet.

'Come!' Butler appeared at my cabin door, where I had returned to pick up my belongings. 'The ship is sailing into harbour at last. We will be first down the gangplank!'

I kept up my courage as we went on deck for the last time, shaking hands with Bill Carthy, who wished me luck, and coming face to face with Jack Miller, who broke away from his family to join me.

'This is a sad parting, Annie!' he declared, defying my father to come and talk to me. 'America is a vast land, and who knows where Fortune will take us?'

I drank in my last sight of Jack's friendly face, which was no longer ordinary to me, but interesting and precious in its every angle and shadow. I marked the shapes and colours in my mind's eye, to recall them whenever I could. 'I will miss you, Jack,' I said simply.

'Enough!' Butler snapped, drawing me away. His attention was on the wooden wharf and the bustle of figures there.

And now we could hear the sound of voices above the creak of the ship's timbers. Sailors heaved down the sails and threw ropes down to the wharf where they were secured. Passengers crowded against the rail, eager to set foot on land.

'Who are all the people?' I heard Maggie ask her father.

We could see lines of men staring up at the deck. They were well dressed in long jackets and white wigs, for all the world like gentlemen back home.

'They are the planters,' her father replied, 'come to buy slaves and take servants.'

'Shall we be slaves?' Maggie asked, clutching the little doll Jack had carved for her.

'No, and not servants either. We shall be free men,' Matthew Miller said, turning to watch Trapp bring up the convicts from down below. 'These are the wretches who will be sold as slaves.'

I heard Butler swear under his breath at the sound of their rattling chains. He pulled me towards the place where the gangplank was set against the side of the ship.

'Stand back!' Trapp ordered, leading the prisoners towards the narrow plank.

Most passengers gave way for the wretches, but Butler had his pressing reason to go ahead of them. He stepped with me on to the plank, which shook unsteadily.

'Mister Butler!' Captain Andrews shouted from his high deck. 'Sir, you must let the prisoners go before you!'

'I will let no man tell me what to do!' my father shouted back, pushing me ahead down the slope.

The men in chains followed, making the plank shake more, so that I feared I would fall sideways into the dock.

'Hurry!' Butler urged.

At last I stepped on to the wharf and was swallowed by the crowd of waiting gentlemen. I saw that most were young, with weathered faces like those of sailors, and though they dressed finely, they had the broad hands of farmers.

Here is my chance! I thought, as Butler stopped by the edge of the wharf and called for his chest to be carried down.

I slipped between two of the Virginian planters, planning to flee in any direction, no matter where.

But one of the gentlemen caught hold of me and

said I must wait for my father. 'Child, do not venture off alone,' he warned. 'This is a strange country to you. Your father must take care not to let you out of his sight.'

I groaned inwardly as he took my hand and pushed me back towards Butler, who still called for his chest, which contained all his ill-gotten possessions. But the convicts still came down the plank, and the chest was carried behind them, until the last prisoner turned suddenly and without warning, violently rocking the walkway and making the sailors sway with their heavy burden.

'Take heed!' Butler cried, running forward to watch helplessly as the sailors at the top of the plank overbalanced and dropped their load.

The chest fell against the plank, balanced for a moment, then toppled into the water, where it sank from sight.

There was a gasp and a cry from all who saw. But the convict at the end of the line laughed and raised his chains above his head with his left arm. The right hung limp and useless at his side.

Unthank! I knew in an instant that the man was about to take his revenge against Butler. Again I tried to slip away, but this time it was Butler who caught me by the hand.

He stared aghast into the gurgling water, at the spot where his wealth had vanished.

And it was I who said we must go, forget what we had lost, and make haste away. 'For pity's sake, leave it!' I begged.

But anger devoured him. Dragging me with him, he struggled past the line of convicts who were stepping from the plank one by one, until he came to the triumphant, laughing figure of the man who would ruin us. He seized him and pulled him on to the wharf, taking a knife from the underside of his coat and pressing it against Unthank's throat.

'Stop!' I cried, wrenching at Butler's arm.

He threw me down on to the ground, amongst the feet of the planters.

'Mister Butler, put away the knife!' Trapp called, striding forward at last.

'His name is not Butler!' Unthank sneered. With a future as a slave before him, he did not care about the knife at his throat.

'Put away the knife!' Trapp shouted a second time, seeing that Butler twisted it in his hand, ready to push it home.

Then, from nowhere, there was a loud, sharp shot from a gun and Butler fell back.

I looked up at Captain Andrews, his pistol aimed steady at Butler's head, the barrel still smoking.

I looked down in horror at the blood oozing from my tormentor's temple.

'His name is Thomas Hague!' Unthank proclaimed

in a triumphant voice, looking down at the bleeding corpse. 'The girl is Maggie Nightingale. As God is my witness, they killed five men to escape the noose at York!'

Two

I fled through the broad streets of Jamestown into the forest. Men pursued me, but fear drove me on and I outran them at last.

I flung myself down in a secluded place, beneath the pine trees, on damp, sweet-smelling earth. For a long time my breath came short and my chest ached.

Then, when my breath was easier, I raised my head and looked around. The giant trees rose straight, their trunks rough, the branches forming a high canopy. It was so quiet and still that it seemed that no man had set foot here before me.

I turned to lie on my back, still fearing the sounds of pursuit. Were those footsteps I had heard? And did I see movement between the tall trunks? I listened and watched.

Soon creatures came down from the trees – I knew that some were squirrels, but others, with black and white banded tails, I did not recognise. Birds hopped along the soft ground towards me, their bright blue wings catching in the light. I closed my eyes and took a deep breath.

So, Thomas Hague my tormentor was dead and I had inherited a dreadful legacy in the shape of the hangman's noose. The long voyage across the ocean had been in vain – I was no more safe now than I had been in old England!

In many ways, my plight was worse, for I was friendless and alone. There was no Mally Truefit to tell me to be brave, no neighbours who would give me shelter, no one who cared whether I lived or died.

And for a while I myself had no thought for survival, lying a good while on the ground, until the creatures grew bold and ran close to me, gathering food. Then I got to thinking that my case might not be so bad as I had thought. So, Unthank had taken his revenge and named me alongside Hague, but if this was indeed a vast country, as men said, then surely I might travel a distance to a place where none had heard my name.

I will shun the towns I said to myself, picking myself up from the ground at last. *I will make my appearance plain, so that none will think me a lady, and I will walk through the country until I come to a farm which may want a servant.*

So thinking, I took up my satchel and opened it, choosing a blue skirt and a dark green bodice and putting on my simplest linen. Then I let down my hair and braided it plainly, satisfied that I was altered enough and might walk along without recognition.

But whither should I walk? Each way I turned, the forest seemed to last for ever, growing darker the further I stepped into it, until I soon lost all sense of which way I had come. However, a glimpse of sun through the dark canopy guided me south and west, and I took comfort when I found a clearing with a stream and found myself in the company of a small herd of deer.

The creatures bounded away when they saw me, leaving me alone again and curious about tree-trunks which lay at the edge of the clearing, chopped down and stored there for some purpose. This meant that men lived nearby and I decided to go on more cautiously.

I must walk further, I told myself. Perhaps for two or three days, before I show myself and set about seeking work. I hoped that by then I would be safe.

But this meant spending nights in the forest, and I was not brave enough to do this without a great deal of trepidation.

In fact, my heart sank with the sun and I grew very low. I thought every shadow threatened me and every boulder hid the man who would leap out and declare my condemned name. Then it grew cold and I sought shelter under a low thorn bush, breaking branches and pulling them around me so that creatures such as wolves and bears would not disturb me during the night. *Will there be wolves?* I wondered, wrapping my cloak around me, wishing I was still on board the *Good Endeavour*. I stayed awake many hours, shivering and watching.

It grew light at last and I found myself in want of food. I knew I would find none in the forest and so I picked a direction where the trees seemed to grow thinner and might give way to bushes that bore fruit such as the blue berries that grew on the moors back home. *The men who chopped the trees must live off the land* I thought to myself, not knowing how soon my curiosity was to be answered.

I walked on towards what I took to be another clearing, but had not reached it before two men appeared from between the trees and approached me.

These men were like none I had ever seen. They wore only skins draped around their waists, with shoes made of the same leather. Their chests and arms were streaked with white, grey and black patterns There were strings of beads and shells around their necks and feathers in their long, dark hair.

I saw them and turned to flee. But there was another behind me, and now I saw still others approaching silently, some carrying knives and long spears.

I could not run, so I stood instead and waited for the first two men to come close, trembling and fearing that they meant to kill me.

They came up to me and walked around me, surveying me with suspicion. One reached out to touch the stuff of my skirt. Then they spoke rapidly to each other in a language I did not know, though the sounds were like the bubbling of a stream over rocks and wind through trees.

I watched the men, wary as the deer who had run from the clearing, gradually coming to believe that I need not fear them, for they talked a long time without offering me violence, then turned and pointed me which way I should go. They walked beside me, their companions keeping their distance, until we did at last come to the clearing in the forest.

I went with my strange new friends to a small stream that ran between rocks, stooping to drink the pure water. Afterwards, the men showed me berries which I might eat and watched me devour them hungrily. They spoke again, as if deciding what they should do next, standing well away from me and still regarding me with open curiosity.

I ate my fill and then thanked them. I offered them my hand in a gesture of gratitude then pointed at what I took to be my way ahead, though I had no sense of my journey's end.

One of the men, whose face was streaked with red as well as white, shook his head and turned me in another direction.

I nodded and thanked him again. Now I began to

fear that they would not let me leave and so hurried to set off. But I had not gone twenty steps when the same man came up alongside me and walked with me, not uttering any words, but looking and nodding and settling into the rhythm of my steps. Glancing behind, I saw that the other men were satisfied to see him go with me.

He is my guide! I thought in surprise. And somehow I trusted the man who walked beside me, though his painted face was like a mask and he looked straight ahead. *He will take me out of the forest!*

Understanding that I had no wish to go back the way I had come but wanted to put a great distance behind me, this man travelled with me for two days and nights through the strange land, stopping to show me where to find food and water, carrying me on his back over streams and helping me to climb rocks when we came to them. Once he stopped to catch fish in a wide river, building a fire out of wood and cooking the white flesh to share with me. We slept soundly at night, under the stars.

I never knew his name, or where he came from, but I thank him for leading me and treating me kindly – a girl he did not know, whom he would not see again.

At the end of the third day we came to the edge of the forest. The land opened out into a wide plain with mountains in the far distance.

My companion stopped and looked out at the plain, waiting for me to see that there were cattle grazing in the shallow valley, and a thin trail of smoke rising from what I took to be a chimney. There were fences to contain the cattle and small plots of cultivated ground scattered here and there.

I nodded and smiled at my unnamed friend. We said farewell in my old country's way, taking each other by the hand and shaking solemnly. 'Thank you,' I said from my heart.

He turned and walked back into the forest.

I went on alone, out into the sunlight, heading for the trail of smoke that rose into the blue sky. I felt as though I had walked through the forest out of my tormented past into a clear future.

That future started with ploughed fields, a horse tethered to a post and a man resting against a gate. 'Lord above!' he said when he saw me approach.

I was a strange figure in this land – a slight girl with dark brown hair, covered in dust and the stains of the forest, walking alone into a new life.

'Where did you spring from?' the man asked, vaulting the gate to stand beside me.

'I am looking for work as a maid servant,' I replied. 'I do not mind where I live or what I do.'

'Oh, you don't?' He studied me closely. 'We don't have much call for maid servants, only farm-hands.'

I held back, trying to take in his appearance, which

reminded me of Bill Carthy, only this man was fair and not dark. Still, he had the same wiry figure and lively features.

'I am Seth Walters,' he said, still eyeing me up and down. 'I live with my wife, Grace, and my son, Jim, here in the valley.'

'My name is Maggie,' I said, leaving behind the lies and deceit. 'I can do farm work, or any kind of work, and I will do my best to serve you.'

'I think you will!' he said with a nod. 'Even though you are young, I see that you mean what you say.'

I waited, hoping with all my heart that my troubles were over and I was safe at last.

'Our farm is small,' he warned, walking me down a track towards a plain wooden house. 'I bought fifty acres from the governor of Virginia two years ago. The first year we cleared and enclosed the land. Last year we planted tobacco. This year Grace gave birth to our son.'

I gazed at the house with its curling smoke, its small windows and long porch. I saw sunflowers growing by the door, and a woman standing with a baby in her arms.

'Come, Maggie, meet my wife and have supper with us,' Seth said. 'Tell us about yourself. If we like you, we surely have work that you can do.'

Three

Grace Walters welcomed me into her house and gave me bread and meat. She asked me how many days I had walked.

'Three,' I replied, telling her that I had been guided through the forest by a man wearing only skins about his waist and feathers in his hair.

The young wife glanced at her husband, who told me that the man belonged to a tribe of natives called the Algonquins who hunted and farmed alongside the white settlers. 'They are proud people,' he explained. 'Lately they grow suspicious of the planters, lest we take more of their land.'

'They did me no harm,' I said, eating my fill.

'Because you intended them no ill,' Grace pointed out, looking firmly at Seth. 'You went peacefully through their forest, and so they were your friends.'

I saw there was a division between the husband and wife – that she defended the natives and that he was suspicious of them. And I noticed a blunderbuss propped against the wall of the log cabin, and a silver pistol lying on the oak chest.

'And now, Maggie, you must tell your story,' Seth insisted, drawing his chair back from the table and taking out a pipe of tobacco. 'Here in the New World we are accustomed to strange sights, but it is not every day that a girl walks alone out of the forest!'

It was the moment I had feared, for though I did not intend to go forward in deceit and trickery, yet I was not prepared to tell the whole truth. 'I sailed from Gravesend, hoping to make a new life,' I began cautiously.

'Alone?' Grace broke in. She went to pick up the crying baby from his cot and walked rhythmically around the room to quieten him.

'No, but my father died,' I told them, close to the truth and yet evading it. 'I found I must make my own way and so I set out from Jamestown to look for work.'

'Poor child!' Grace sighed. She was a small woman with fair hair like her husband, though her movements were slower and more gentle. In her grey dress and plain white collar, I thought she was perhaps a Quaker or some such. 'Do you have any family at all?'

'Not in this world,' I replied.

'Well, you have a stout heart!' Seth praised me. 'Many would not have gone forward, as you did.'

'I can work,' I promised him again and offering to take the baby from Grace. She handed him to me and watched me closely. 'I can cook and clean. I will learn to dig and plant and plough if you wish!'

Silently I prayed that these people would take me in, for I liked them and their quiet manner and the way they had of saying what was in their hearts.

Seth smiled. 'Can you ride a horse, Maggie?'

'A little.'

'Can you sew?' Grace asked me.

'Plain work,' I replied. 'I will sew dainty clothes for the baby out of petticoats I carry with me and make silk curtains for the windows out of skirts I will wear no more!'

'The girl is a wonder!' Seth laughed, noticing that baby Jim lay quietly in my arms. 'Can you sing a lullaby, Maggie?'

'Only give me place at your hearth and you shall hear me sing!' I promised.

At this, both smiled and told me to be easy in my mind.

'Stay with us,' Grace said kindly. 'You are no longer an orphan, Maggie, but part of our small family. Sleep, and in the morning we will show you our farm.'

Strange, my life of late had been stormy and full of trouble, but now I fell into an easeful time of sunshine and calm.

Seth Walters' word was good. The day after I arrived, he put me on a horse and rode with me around his land, showing me the tall, broad-leaved tobacco crop yellowing under the fierce sun, and fields of wheat and maize. 'We keep cattle for our milk and cheese, and chickens for eggs. We have a barn for drying the tobacco.'

I gazed around and saw that all was orderly. 'Does your land go as far as the mountains?' I asked, pointing to the hazy blue hills in the distance.

Seth smiled and said that others owned land in the valley besides him. 'Last year my neighbour bought a parcel of land beyond the river for thirty-five guineas. His wife has bought him a long wig and a silver-hilted sword, and now he swaggers about the country like a fine gentleman!'

I laughed with Seth and said he must buy a wig and ride a fine horse if he were to keep up. 'Who owned the land before your neighbour bought it?' I asked.

'The governor of Virginia has a map showing thousands of acres of land which the King of England wishes him to sell.'

'And may any man begin to plant?' I thought then of my friends the Millers and of how they must apply to the governor. And I wondered whether Matthew Miller had the means to buy a good parcel of land. Then I regretted the loss of Butler's sea chest containing his bank-notes, gold coins and silver plate, knowing now that I could have used it to help my friends, both old and new.

'Any man may settle here provided he has the money to pay,' Seth answered. 'And that is why I look ahead and see trouble with the natives, whose families have lived here for many years, and they say their fathers' spirits live in those mountains and watch over them.'

But I looked around me and could not imagine men fighting over this beautiful land, of which there seemed so much – enough for all, as I thought.

I soon learned to till the soil. Many days I spent under the sun wearing a broad straw hat and a plain calico apron over my blue skirt. The tall green tobacco plants turned to gold and Seth, Grace and I harvested them, stacking them on a cart and driving the horse back across the open valley. We cut down the wheat and threshed it, we fed the maize to the cattle.

With Grace I baked bread and preserved berries in stone bottles. The house smelled sweet as we drifted towards autumn.

And at night I would sit with Jim on the porch, humming softly, looking out at the open sky, where a million stars twinkled. '*Hush-a-bye baby*,' I sang. He stared up at me, lulled by the motion of my rocking chair. '*Hush-a-bye baby in the treetop, When the wind blows the cradle will rock . . .*'

A million stars in the heavens – the same stars I had gazed at during my long voyage across the ocean, the same heavens where my true father rested in peace.

'When the bough breaks the cradle will fall. Down will come baby, cradle and all.'

Sometimes, as the days grew colder, the natives would pass by when I worked in Seth's fields. They carried wood for their fires, the carcases of deer they had hunted. The men would stop and look towards me, perhaps knowing the story of how I had walked alone through the forest. And I would stop my work, straighten my back and gaze at their painted faces, hoping to see the man who had guided me, but I never did.

Then Seth would come and stand beside me, his legs wide apart, hands on his hips. The native men would turn and walk on.

'They say their gods live in the mountains and speak with the voices of their dead fathers,' Seth told me after one of these chance meetings. 'They have no churches or meeting houses.'

It is enough I thought. I wished the voice of my own father would speak to me from the mountains.

And in any case, there was one day in the week which I did not enjoy while I lived with my new family, and this was the Sabbath when we went by horse and cart across the plain to meet fellow Quakers for silent prayer.

Each Sunday we would wash and dress in fresh linen and drive out together, Grace holding Jim, and me sitting beside Seth at the front of the cart. I would stare into the sky, watching eagles soar high above, noticing each week that the wind blew colder and the fields grew barer. We drew up outside a neighbour's cabin, sometimes close under the shadow of the mountains, sometimes at the edge of the forest, once at the house of the neighbour whose wife wished to turn him into a gentleman.

'So this is your new servant!' the wife cried, spying me on the cart and rushing to meet us. 'Oh, Grace, it is a pretty thing that God has sent you!'

I frowned, thinking it was not God but the devil Hague who brought me here and that if God had any part to play, it was in keeping my secret safe. Then I climbed down to the ground, unwilling to let the people stare at me. There were new faces and new names, prying eyes and men who thought they must ask questions about where I originated and how I came to be here.

'Now, child,' said one, 'how is it that you were cast into the world without shelter?'

'Maggie does not like to talk about it,' Grace explained, leading me by the hand into the house, which was large but plain. 'She has suffered much misfortune in her short life.'

Thus protected, I sat quietly next to her, knowing that we would not sing to praise the Lord or pray out loud to him, but would share our thoughts simply. I had grown used to their plain worship and so I sat throughout lost in my own thoughts and was glad enough when we climbed in our cart and returned home.

Some days later, I was sitting alone in the porch in the early evening when I heard the beat of a horse's hoofs and looked up to see a man approaching our cabin. Closer to, I saw that it was our gentleman neighbour dressed in a fine black coat and feathered hat, riding in a new saddle complete with a holster for his shining pistol.

The man stopped before the house, jumped down to the ground and threw me his horse's reins. He strode past me without greeting.

'I have lately come from Jamestown!' I heard him tell Grace as he entered the house. 'Where is Seth? I would speak with him on an urgent matter.'

Overhearing this, I felt my heart flutter, then quieted it and reminded myself that our neighbour could mean any number of things.

'Seth is repairing fences on our eastern boundary,' Grace told him, inviting the man to tell her the business.

'No,' he replied, 'I will seek him out and speak to him man to man.'

'Very well, neighbour,' Grace said, walking out on to the porch with the visitor, who glanced afresh at me with such a look in his eyes that I knew in an instant what the matter was.

'What does the girl call herself?' he asked Grace in an aside.

'Her name is Maggie.'

He nodded and snatched his horse's reins from me. 'Maggie,' he echoed, as if satisfied. 'Child, I think we have met before!'

Saying not another word, he mounted his horse and rode off to find Seth.

How could we meet? I asked myself, my throat turning dry and my head beginning to swim.

'He means that he saw you last Sunday when we prayed at his house, does he not?' Grace asked with a puzzled look.

I had the man's face still before my eyes – the straight brow, square jaw, lines about his eyes made by strong sunlight. And then I recalled the scene where I had seen him.

I stood on the bustling wharf next to the *Good Endeavour*. Butler called for his sea chest and I slipped away into the crowd of planters waiting to buy slaves, intending to flee. A man's broad hand had fallen upon my shoulder. 'Child, do not venture off alone,' he had said. And the features of that man were those of our inquisitive neighbour!

'Why must he talk with Seth?' Grace wondered, staring after the galloping figure.

I ran inside the house, up the ladder and into the loft which was used to store grain, a corner of which contained my bed. I sank to the floor beside a sack of wheat and for a full minute shock prevented me from stirring.

'Maggie?' Grace called from down below. 'Are you sick? What ails you?'

Her voice brought me back to myself and I called an answer as best I could.

'Yes, I am sick,' I replied. 'It is a fever in my head.'

'Lie down. I will find herbs to soothe you.'

'No. Leave me. I will rest here.'

I heard Grace set foot on the ladder and then the sound of the baby stirring and beginning to cry.

'Hush!' Grace soothed, going away and leaving me to myself.

And now I must put my few belongings into my satchel and leave the house before Seth and our neighbour returned. This could be done without Grace's knowledge if I flung my bag to the ground from the opening to the loft which overlooked the yard at the back of the cabin and then climbed after it down a ladder resting against the outside wall.

So while the good mother tended to her baby I quickly carried out my plan, and was gone well before sunset, picking up my satchel and running swiftly away from the cabin, into the shelter of willow bushes growing by a stream. Here I crouched and caught my breath.

I should not have looked back at the little house with the smoke curling from the chimney, its logs for the winter neatly stacked in the yard. I should not have hesitated and thought how happy I might have been, living there, for my heart almost broke when I saw it for the last time and I scarce had strength to go on.

But then I heard the sound of horses and knew that Seth was returning, full of our neighbour's news from the Jamestown wharf. Once more I felt the brand of thief and murderer sink into my flesh and heard the echo of Unthank's triumphant voice condemning me the very moment I set foot into the New World.

Four

I ran then, back into the forest whence I had come, away from my Quaker friends who now thought me wicked beyond redemption.

I fled and the tall trees swallowed me, their shadows closing around me.

A darkness fell upon me that night like none I had lived through before. It was not the blackness of the forest, but of the soul – a despair that oppressed me and made me sink to the ground, careless of whether I lived or died. For Fate had dealt me a cruel hand, and though I had fought against it with all the courage and wit I could gather, still Fate beat me down again, robbing me of my friends and pitching me always into loneliness.

So I lay in the forest throughout the night, almost senseless, feeling the cold dew settle upon me at sunrise, still robbed of the will to move.

Rays of the sun began to filter through the thick branches high overhead. Blue jays flew from branch to branch. A mother deer and her fawn passed close by.

What is left for me to do? I asked myself as I lay curled on my side. *I have tried to make my life anew, I have worked hard and honestly as any man may, and yet I cannot escape my past!*

And I thought it would have been better if I had sailed the ocean in chains and lived in the hold with the convicts, because at least they knew their fate, which was to be sold as slaves and to live henceforth as labourers in the field. Whereas I had no place in the world, not even with the lowest of mankind, and was cast out into the forest to live like an animal, always afraid, always fleeing from my enemies.

The sun crept through the branches and touched my face. I felt its soft rays. And for a reason I could not fathom, their warmth moved me and I began to weep, raising myself from the ground until I stood, trembling and sobbing as though my heart would break.

Then my old friends, the natives of the forest, walked out from behind the trees and approached me, holding out their hands. They took me up and carried me until we came to an Algonquin camp with a long house built of wood with tall trunks supporting the structure and a fire in the middle of the house whose smoke rose through a hole in the roof.

The fire flickered red and welcoming, and the man who carried me set me down beside it.

Then women came with soft fur blankets, which they wrapped around me, and they gave me water to drink and flat bread to eat, stroking my head, wiping away my tears and speaking strange, kind words. And children surrounded me and nestled close – some of the smallest ones wholly naked save for a string of wooden beads around their necks, all with straight, black hair glossy as a bird's wing.

I felt the fire warm me, heard the men speak with the women, often pointing at me, so that I began to wonder what they meant to do with me.

'Do not send me back to the valley!' I pleaded with one of the women. 'The people there do not want me!'

She held my hand, puzzled by the babble of sound that fell from my lips. She spoke back with a gentle expression, offering me sweet fruits to eat, gesturing that I should lay my head down on one of the blankets and take my rest. She smiled as I did so, softly touching the frill of lace I wore on my cuffs and the supple, shiny leather of my shoes.

Feeling easier, I lay on the blanket, gazing round at the large wicker baskets standing in line along the sides of the rough walls and at the animal skins stretched out to dry on wooden frames. By the wide door I saw a narrow wooden boat, pointed at both ends, painted with white and red zigzag patterns.

Outside the door, two men fashioned another boat.

All this was strange to me, but comfortable. I rested to the sounds of children playing and women grinding maize between flat stones, while the men outside hammered and whittled at the wood. The day passed without incident.

Then at night the man who had carried me into the camp came and took me to a fire in the open air where meat was cooked and a meal eaten. All looked at me with open curiosity, and I stared back at their wild locks and painted bodies, wondering what the marks might signify, noticing that they all listened respectfully to an old man with white hair plainly braided and hanging to each side of his lined face.

The old man studied me closely as I ate. He ordered the women to give me more meat than I could eat, raising his hand and motioning that I should draw nearer to him. Then he looked deep into my eyes, as if he could read the strange story of my life there, nodded once and murmured a few words to my rescuer, who was tallest and strongest of the men around the fire.

Though I could not understand the old man, I saw him to mean that he was satisfied by what he saw in my eyes by the way the tall man nodded at me and smiled.

'Eat!' he said in his own language, gesturing with his hands.

I motioned back that my stomach was already full, and the men laughed and told the women to take me back to the house, where again they made me comfortable.

And for the first time I knew that the dreadful events that had befallen me need not play a part in my life with these people, for they could ask me no questions and judged me only by what they saw in my eyes, and what they read there seemed to please them and they were kind to me.

I settled there, afraid only that the outside world would come crashing in, for there were signs that the native people grew wary as autumn gave way to winter, when there was less food and they must go further abroad to bring back meat and fish.

Men would set out each morning armed with spears and bows and arrows, either on foot or by boat along the nearby river, which must be the same river that flowed through the plain where the white planters farmed. It was broad and slow, its banks clogged by reeds.

Sometimes I would stand at the edge of the trees, watching the hunters wade into the brown water then jump into their canoes, paddling upstream towards deserted areas of the forest where the deer roamed freely. Once, at the end of the day, I watched them return with the carcase of a brown and white beast which I recognised as that of a cow – one which had perhaps strayed from the farmed land into the forest, where the natives had killed it. The sight sent a shudder through me, reminding me that my enemies were not far away after all.

Soon autumn faded into winter. Days grew short, nights were long and cold. Snow came.

And with it the farmers. They rode on horseback into the forest with axes to fell the trees for building more barns and for firewood. I stayed with the women and children within the longhouse, but I could hear their axes and their voices calling familiar words. Our men would steal out to watch those who trampled through their forest. They carried with them spears and knives, but they did not attack the planters, who did not see them or know that they were being watched. At the end of the day the farmers would tie ropes around the trunks they had felled and use their horses to drag them away.

At these times, I took care not to walk out and be seen, but there was one unlucky day when I had strayed alone to the riverbank to gather reeds for the baskets which the women had taught me to weave. It was a clear day, towards the end of the afternoon.

Bending over to cut the reeds, I did not notice a boat with two settlers in it float silently downstream towards me until they had drawn level and were close enough to see my startled features.

'Look there!' one of the men said, picking up a rifle and aiming at me. It was the first time that I had heard words spoken in my own tongue for many weeks.

'It's the convict girl, I'll be bound!' said the other, seeing me turn my back and a get ready to flee. 'Our neighbour says there is a warrant out for her and a reward of ten guineas, dead or alive!'

I ran from them, my back turned to the gun, stumbling clumsily over the wet ground.

I heard a shot, was amazed to find myself not hit and still fleeing towards the forest.

'Fire again!' I heard one of the men cry.

There was another shot and still I was on my feet, running. Gasping, I gained the cover of the forest, darting behind the nearest trunk and not moving until I was sure that the men in the boat had lost sight of me.

Then my native friends came running through the forest at the sound of gunfire – ten or more of them appearing as if from nowhere, drawing back the strings of their bow and firing arrows at the boat.

The farmers shouted oaths but did not stop to fight. Instead they took up their oars and rowed away as fast as they could, for though they longed for the reward, they were not prepared to risk their lives for it.

After this day, fear came back to me, and I did not live an instant without looking over my shoulder at who might be following me or wondering when one of the settlers might come to claim his reward.

I slept uneasily, and my days were full of dread. I could speak to no one about it, only trust that my friends in the forest would keep faith with me and protect me again if men from the valley came back to hunt me out.

Indeed, they took care to see that I did not wander

out of the camp alone, and the old chief told the women to keep me close in the longhouse until winter was done.

So my days passed in weaving reeds and in grinding corn, sometimes singing for my companions songs from the old world of noble Robin Hood who robbed the rich to help the poor and of the mermaid whose siren song tempted poor sailors on to the rocks.

The women seemed to like the curious notes and the sweet sound of my voice. The children would always clamour for more.

One night, however, I was more than usually troubled and I rose from my low bed and went to sit by the glowing embers of the fire. It was the sad song of Geordie that came into my mind then, of how the lady called for her milk-white horse to ride and plead for the life of the man she loved and how she saw him hanged in golden chains in spite of her pleas. I hummed the tune without forming the words, staring into the dying fire.

A noise from outside the house broke into my thoughts and straight away I was afraid. I had heard what sounded like a twig snapping underfoot – perhaps only an animal straying too close to camp after all, and nothing to wake the others over. Then it came again – a brittle crack, then silence. With my heart beating fast, I crept towards the door.

I had only peered outside for a moment, at trodden snow lying underfoot and a full moon up above, when I felt someone seize me and place a hand over my mouth. I kicked and struggled, trying to raise the alarm, but my kidnapper swiftly carried me off towards the trees, where an accomplice waited with two horses.

'Help me!' I cried out, as the first man slung me across his horse and leaped into the saddle.

My cry woke the sleeping natives, who came running with spears and knives. The riders turned their horses roughly and set off away from the camp.

'Let me go, I have done you no wrong!' I pleaded, sorely jolted by the movement of the horse, feeling the trees perilously close to my hanging head.

My kidnapper and his companion swore at their mounts and forced them on. Behind us, the men of the tribe threw their spears and did not give up their pursuit.

Then, all of a sudden, a figure stepped into our path and the moon cast a long shadow before us. Startled, the horses reared. I felt myself slip to the snowy ground and saw the two riders thrown clear.

A spear landed not far away.

'Annie!' a voice said.

I looked up to see one whom I thought I would never see again, but whose features were etched in my mind. It was Jack Miller, bending over me, begging me to stand and run with him, away from the kidnappers, who had recovered and now seized pistols from their saddle holsters.

My eyes started from my head, I drew breath in short, sharp gasps.

'Ask no questions. Run!' Jack told me.

My Algonquin friends were almost upon the two kidnappers, and before they could aim their pistols, they had surrounded them within a circle of sharp spears.

'Do not fire!' I begged the two men, darting towards them. I could not leave my friends in danger, though my own life depended on it.

They paused and glanced at me, and in that second the natives threw themselves upon them, wresting their guns from their hands and throwing them to the ground while their frightened horses bolted.

Then I ran to the tallest of my friends, the man who had found me and carried me into the camp many weeks before, and pulled him away from the kidnappers, telling him not to harm them but to send them on their way, for I would not have men killed because of me.

He understood and made the other natives stand back, marching the two men with four of his natives to the edge of the forest, from where they must find their own way home.

Meanwhile I picked myself up from the snow and put my hands over my eyes, thinking that Jack Miller was a ghost and not a real figure standing before me. I looked again – he was still there.

'Annie,' he began, keeping a wary eye on the wild figures of my native rescuers. 'The two men who pursued you intend to drag you back to Jamestown. They will return and seize you, dead or alive, believe me!'

'And you – what do you mean to do?' I asked in a faint voice.

'They want to see you hanged!' he insisted. 'I heard them making their plan in town and followed them here in secret.'

'Jack!' I implored. 'Tell me what you are doing here. Do not leave me in doubt a moment longer!'

At which Jack Miller looked calmly at me in the moonlight, in the middle of the forest, surrounded by men armed with spears. 'I mean to save your life,' he said in his plain, honest way. 'But now I see you have other friends to assist you!'

Five

'My father has bought land in Carolina,' Jack explained. 'I have helped him clear the forest and build a house. But when winter came I asked if I might leave the family for a time and sail back across Chesapeake Bay.'

We sat in the longhouse, by the last embers of the fire. As dawn rose, our native friends stood guard at the door.

'Why did you come back to Jamestown?' I asked.

Jack's steady gaze held me. 'To find you,' he answered. 'I knew you were in danger and wished to get away earlier, but my father had need of me.'

'You came to help a convict condemned to hang,' I told him. 'For it is true, Jack. My name is Maggie Nightingale.'

'And that was the dark secret you kept from me during our long sea voyage,' he reminded me. 'It was the hold that Butler had over you.'

'Not Butler, but Thomas Hague, the notorious smuggler!' Even his name filled me with dread. 'Did he indeed die from the captain's bullet?'

Jack nodded. 'But they recovered his sea chest. Captain Andrews had it hauled up from the bed of the harbour. It was full of gold and silver plate!'

'Hah! And all of it counterfeit, like the man himself!' I smiled at this then shuddered. 'And what of the convict, Dick Unthank?'

Jack paused a while, looking around at his surroundings, grinning and winking at the curious faces of the small children peering out from behind the tall woven baskets. 'Unthank's broken arm healed in time,' he replied. 'I know this for a certainty because my father sailed into Jamestown to buy provisions before winter set in and he sought out the man. He has employed him on our Carolina plantation. In time he will earn a certificate of discharge and be free to go where he wishes.'

'That is a good ending,' I murmured, glad for Unthank's change of fortune, but still seeing Hague's bleeding corpse stretched out on the wharf in my mind's eye.

Jack's penetrating gaze missed nothing. 'You have suffered much,' he said quietly.

I bowed my head. 'I am condemned to death for a crime I did not commit,' I told him. 'My life has been taken up by a hard-hearted villain and wrenched from its allotted path down dark alleys and turnings which have taken me far from home. Hague has made me a fugitive in two worlds – the old and the new. Worst of all, I lost my dear father because of him.'

'But look up, Maggie!' Jack said. 'Look around you now. You have found friends in a place you would least expect!'

'I have met with nothing but kindness here,' I confessed, inviting one of the small girls to sit in my lap while her mother rebuilt the fire. 'And now you, Jack, have sought me out, even though people said I was wicked and fit for nothing but the hangman's noose.'

'People say many things that I cannot believe,' he replied. 'Back in the old world, rich men say that poor men deserve only hovels to live in. Men of the church say that a sinner may not enter heaven and yet bishops live off the fat of the land while the rest starve.'

I shook my head nervously. 'Hush!'

'Who can hear us?' he laughed. 'Besides, we are in a country where all start with nothing, and only the honest and industrious thrive. There is much unclaimed land here, Maggie – rich soil and long, hot summers! The sky is so big and empty you would think it went on for ever!'

'You have grown strong, Jack,' I said, noticing that he was taller and broader than when I had last seen him on board the *Endeavour*. 'It seems you like the New World and all it has to offer.' I spoke a little sadly, thinking of my own wretched situation. Still I could not believe that his friendship with me was so strong that it had brought him back from his new life in search of a condemned creature such as me.

'And so shall you!' he promised, standing up and striding towards the door where two men still kept watch.

I set down the child and followed him, hesitating to stand beside him and so hanging back a little. 'I want to tell you how I came to be condemned,' I began. 'Then you may judge me truly and tell me if I have indeed done any wrong.'

Jack walked out into the clearing and stood with his arms folded, staring up into the high trees. 'I know that you have lived in fear and sorrow for too long, Maggie. And I am certain that you have a pure heart.'

'*How* do you know?' I insisted.

He smiled. 'Firstly, I have studied you closely. Secondly, my mother is fond of you and she has sound judgment. Thirdly, I have heard you sing!'

'What has that to do with it?' I protested, beginning to smile in spite of myself.

'You sing with your soul,' he declared. 'A pure voice such as yours never came out of meanness and vice!'

'You are very sure!' I laughed. 'I must remember to tell that to the judge!'

Which remark brought us back to seriousness, for there was a grave question mark over my future which even Jack could not answer.

'Do not be down-hearted,' Jack urged. 'Now that I have found you, I can give you news from Jamestown.'

'All news from the town is bad!' I declared, turning away and walking back into the house. 'They offer a reward of ten guineas for my capture. Those two men will be back!'

Jack came after me. 'That much is true,' he admitted. 'But, Maggie, I have spoken to others in the town, and by chance I met Bill Carthy in an inn by the harbour. You remember him?'

I nodded. 'Does he still sail with Captain Andrews?'

'He does. The ship is anchored at present in the Potomac estuary, waiting for fair weather to return to England. But listen, Bill told me of papers that Captain Andrews brought with him on his last voyage.'

'What papers?'

'Papers from the English court, concerning convicts transported during the summer just past. That is all Bill knows for certain, but he believes the names of Thomas Hague and his accomplice Maggie Nightingale are mentioned there.'

I closed my eyes and tried to order my thoughts, but talk of court papers made me faint with fear. 'And is this your news?' I cried, backing away from Jack, attracting the attention of the women in the longhouse.

Jack frowned. 'Bill thinks the papers may be of use to you, Maggie.'

'How? How can they help me?' My voice rose; I held out my hands in a gesture of supplication.

'I do not know, but I believe we should return to Jamestown to find out.'

Jack's words sounded like a death sentence to me and I covered my ears in dismay.

'Bill Carthy is an honest man,' Jack insisted. 'He would not betray you. It seems Captain Andrews delivered the papers in person to the governor of Virginia. That is where we must go!'

I shook my head. 'I cannot. I dare not!'

Two of the women came forward to put their arms around my shoulders and turned me away from the visitor who had made me weep. They spoke soothing words, stroking my hair and leading me to the far side of the fire.

'Then I will go alone!' Jack declared, hiding the disappointment he must have felt. 'I will leave you here with your friends, who must guard against the men who came here to seize you. I will return as soon as I can.'

Freeing myself from the women, I walked back to face Jack, whose face glowed in the light of the fire.

I had two choices, I saw now – the first was to go with Jack into the very heart of danger; the second was to wait here like an animal caught in a trap, waiting for my hunters to return.

Taking a deep breath, I looked him in the eye. 'I will

come with you after all,' I decided. 'If my life is to be saved, I myself must play my part!'

My native friends did not want to see me go, and neither did I wish to say farewell. They had welcomed me and treated me kindly, had fed me and kept me warm when all others had abandoned me. I had grown used to their slow, soft movements, their strength and grace.

But the old chief saw that it was time for me to go. He came into the longhouse, walking around Jack in a wide, slow circle, looking him up and down.

Jack did not waver under the strength of the old man's gaze.

Then the chief came and took me by the hand. He led me to Jack and placed my hand in his, sealing our young hands between his gnarled ones and sending us on our way.

The women surrounded us and gave us gifts of bread and meat to take with us. The children tugged at my skirt, begging to be lifted and hugged.

And finally, one of the men gave us a knife whose horn handle was wonderfully carved, its blade encased in a leather sheath decorated with beads and fringes. Jack took it and bowed his head in thanks.

And, as if this was not enough, two other men led us from the clearing towards the river, where a boat lay waiting, into which we stepped. The men followed, taking up the oars and rowing us away from the bank, downstream towards the sea.

In a mixture of sorrow and great apprehension, I turned my head to look back towards the shore. Perhaps I had hoped to give a final wave to the people who had saved my life. But the bank was empty. Only the reeds moved in the cold breeze and a solitary deer stood there, his magnificent antlers touched with frost, his proud head raised to watch us go.

Six

Of the many journeys I had made in the year just past, I believe this was the one I made with the heaviest heart.

It was as if I travelled from freedom into servitude, from the wide open space of the forest into, at best, the narrow confines of a prison cell.

And yet, I told myself I could not have lived any longer a peaceful life with my Algonquin friends, for the secret was out, and this thanks to my own carelessness in collecting reeds by the riverbank when I ought to have looked about me and not strayed from the clearing.

Besides, I had Jack Miller next to me in the boat to give me a grain of courage as we journeyed down-river.

'I do not mean that you should march up to the governor's house and knock at his front door,' he explained to me as we approached the town after a full day and a cold night on the river. 'That would be foolishness. No, we must find a safe place for you close by while I go about the business of discovering the contents of the papers that Bill Carthy talked of.'

'Perhaps we should seek out Captain Andrews instead,' I suggested. 'I know that he lives here in Virginia with his wife and a daughter named Jenny.'

Jack thought a while then shook his head. 'It would be a long search, and the captain may not know what the papers contain, for they will be sealed with wax, to keep out prying eyes.'

'Then how can we be sure that they contain good news?' I asked, feeling my heart sink lower as I caught sight of the first houses built by the riverbank and knew that we had come all too soon to the outermost part of Jamestown. Our boatmen knew it too, for they quickly chose a nearby jetty and rowed towards it, eager to leave us there and be gone.

I stood as we approached the wooden stilts, feeling the boat rock beneath me, waiting for Jack to jump on to the rough, frosty boards and hold out his hand to me. Then I sprang quickly from the canoe, thanked the men and watched them row away.

'Have courage!' Jack urged, hurrying me forward along the jetty and between two wooden houses on to a rough track beyond.

It felt strange to have houses around me again and streets to walk down, though these were nothing like the steep streets of Whitby with their stone houses and hidden alleys, but rather broad ways with low, wide houses set back behind neat gardens, and the land was flat and open all the way into the town.

'What if I am recognised?' I asked Jack, lowering my head before the glances of passers-by. I was conscious of my uncombed hair and stained skirt, and of the fact that the townspeople seemed neat and well dressed by comparison.

'Your fame does not spread as far as you imagine,' Jack replied with a smile. 'Only look ahead and no one will pay the least attention.'

So I tried to take on an air of confidence and not to mind the curious glances as we came into the town. Indeed, the bustle settled my nerves a little, as we encountered boys with laden carts and girls running errands from shop to shop. Then there were ladies being taken by in horse-drawn carriages and men on horseback, wearing richly embroidered jackets and black hats sporting white feathers, quite the fashionable gentlemen from the old world, as it were.

'You see, life goes on!' Jack said, leading the way through the throng. We went between wheelwrights and blacksmiths, shoemakers and furriers, even jewellers and silversmiths, towards a great white building at the end of the town's main street.

I held back to let two riders pass by, separated for a time from Jack who strode on ahead. The riders looked down at me and exchanged glances of a kind that suddenly made me afraid once more. However, they rode on and I was calm again.

'That is the governor's house,' Jack told me, pointing ahead at the white house which sported pillars to either side of its grand entrance and had many low windows stretching to either side. There were wide steps up to the door, which was decorated by a graceful fan-shaped window above.

I had once seen drawings of such houses in a book belonging to my father, who had told me that rich men lived in this style in cities such as York and London, yet it was a surprise to see it here in Virginia, where I had imagined all houses to be built of rough logs from the forest. Its grandeur made me feel small and hopeless once more.

'See how the old world perches on the back of the new!' Jack said, not in the least impressed. 'Listen, Maggie, we must find you somewhere to wait in warmth and safety while I find out what we need to know.'

Holding my breath, I nodded and began to seek out a doorway, seeing a church ahead of us which overlooked the frozen lawn in front of the governor's house. The church had a white wooden steeple and a narrow porch that would protect me from view.

'Good,' Jack said, following the direction of my gaze. He settled me on a bench within the porch and said he would not be long. Then he set off across the lawn.

I watched him go with his firm tread up the steps leading to the door. I saw him take hold of the knocker and let it fall. Then three ladies passing by stopped for a moment to talk. I could not see Jack and when the ladies walked on he was gone.

I counted the minutes, scarcely daring to peer out. A boy with a dog came by, then a solitary gentleman, then two more.

'I have no bad word to say about the girl,' said a familiar voice.

I started then pressed myself into the corner of the porch.

'My wife, Grace, and I found her honest and hardworking.'

It is Seth himself! I thought, my heartbeat quickening.

'You are too trusting, neighbour,' the second man said. 'She fled from your house like a thief in the night.'

It was me they were talking of! Jack had been in the wrong to suppose that my fame had not spread.

'And it was proved beyond doubt that she had sailed here with the murderous smuggler, Thomas Hague!'

'I judge as I find,' Seth insisted. 'And to me she seemed true.'

I had no more time to be grateful for Seth's good opinion, however, for I heard rapid footsteps coming down the street and a shadow was cast across the church doorway.

'Where did they go?' a man asked, coming into sight with his back towards me. 'We have followed them since we saw them on the highway into town. But now we lose them in the throng!'

His companion seemed to stride up and down. 'They came as far as the church.'

'We are sure it was them?'

'I swear on the Holy Bible it was! I would know the girl anywhere, since I seized her from the Algonquins and slung her across my saddle!'

And now my nightmare began again, within sight of the governor's house, as I cowered in the church porch, with no Jack to protect me. What should I do? Where should I go?

I had run many times and must do so again!

Turning, I softly opened the church door and stepped inside. All was quiet and calm within, until a lady in a fine crimson dress and wearing a cloak of velvet and fur stood up from kneeling in one of the pews and asked me what I did there.

'I have come to pray!' I replied, my heart pounding within my chest.

She came towards me with a scornful look. 'Child, you are a heathen!' she declared with one look at my ragged clothes. 'Your head is uncovered and your hands unwashed.'

I would have retorted that water would bring me no closer to God, but I bit my tongue, hoping to soften

208

the lady's heart with an honest plea. 'I am being pursued by men who mean to harm me!' I blurted out. 'Please let me take refuge here!'

But she had decided at a glance that I was unworthy and began to push me back towards the open door. 'A dirty little heathen!' said the good Christian woman, giving me one final shove.

And the kidnappers were still outside the church, searching this way and that until they spied me as I was bundled out of the door, when they rushed towards me and tried to seize me once more.

I cried out. People turned to see who made the noise. I darted between my pursuers, into the path of the man who still stood and talked with Seth Walters.

The man blocked my way, so I sidestepped him and ran into Seth himself, who quickly gave way and now prevented his friend from following me.

'Man, she is worth ten guineas, if this be who I think it is!' his companion yelled, only to be pushed aside by the more determined kidnappers.

I began to run across the frosty lawn towards the governor's grand house, like a wild animal overwhelmed by fear who flees into the path of its greatest foe. I heard the men gaining on me, could almost feel their breath upon me.

Then Seth set up a cry of his own. 'Do you mean to kill the poor child!' he roared, setting off in pursuit, quickly catching up and pulling one of the men back.

I saw a glimpse of a pistol in the hand of the other, aimed at me. And then the world slowed almost to a halt, and I thought, *Yes, it is my time to die!* And I felt no fear, only a sense that my trouble was over at last.

But then figures in red coats appeared on the long veranda of the governor's house. The soldiers trained their rifles on the man with the gun. Then a man whom I took to be the governor himself came out with Jack Miller at his side. 'If you shoot, sir, I shall see you hanged!' the governor told my attacker, who let his gun drop to his side.

I stared ahead of me, my sides aching from the thundering of my heart within my chest.

The governor came down the steps and walked towards me, a paper in his hand. 'Are you the girl convict who sailed with Thomas Hague?' he asked.

I looked up into his round, red face which perspired under his full white wig. I tried to read the look in his small, grey eyes that almost vanished beneath heavily hooded lids. 'I am Maggie Nightingale!' I replied, willing myself to hold up my head and not to sink to the ground.

The governor cleared his throat and waved the paper above his head. 'You are the most fortunate girl in the world!' he proclaimed, so that everyone in the crowd could hear. 'I bear a pardon from the King. Break down the gallows, throw open the prison door! Maggie Nightingale, you are innocent of all charges!'

'. . . I am not to be hanged?' I whispered, grasping at Jack, who had run to my side.

He took my hand and led me towards Seth, whose wife and child had joined him outside the governor's house. 'No, Maggie, you are to live!' he said quietly.

And it is Jack's voice telling me this news that I shall remember until the day I die.

Seven

'"I, Solomon Hart, do swear that the girl, Maggie Nightingale, of the Anchor Inn on Saltersgate in the town of Whitby, did not willingly take part in the smuggling of goods from on board the cutter known as the *Eagle* on the 20th day of March in the Year of Our Lord 1756."'

I held the paper in my trembling hand, making out the cramped words with difficulty.

'"On that day, the said Maggie Nightingale was taken prisoner by Thomas Hague, as a safeguard against the girl's father, George Nightingale, betraying him to the Customs Officer on Sandgate, also in Whitby, which said George Nightingale died in the skirmish following upon the attempted arrest of Thomas Hague and his accomplices."' I looked up at Jack, my eyes filled with tears.

'It is signed by Hart and witnessed by James Peacock, the Customs man,' he assured me. 'It seems Mister Peacock drove Hart and a man named Jim Penny to ground some time last summer. He caught them red-handed with kegs of gin stored in the cellars of their houses and forced the truth out of them, on pain of their lives. Then he sent the confession to the York assizes and the judge had it carried to London.'

'This is so.' The governor went on to tell me that the sworn deposition had been carried to him by one of the most honourable men on the high seas, namely Captain Andrews, to whose house he had sent word. 'My serving man delivers a message to the captain even now, to tell him that you have been found.'

It was not long before the tall figure of the sea captain strode towards us, accompanied by his wife and daughter.

'It seems Mister Peacock carried a good opinion of you, Maggie!' Jack said before the captain arrived. 'He did not want to believe you guilty and so went out of his way to prove your innocence.'

Still trembling and trying to hold back my tears, I spoke to the governor. 'Sir, does this mean I may walk away freely?'

'Without a stain on your name, my dear,' he replied, glad for once to perform a happy duty. 'You may go where you please and need never be afraid.'

At this I took a deep breath and clasped Jack's hand.

Then Captain Andrews reached us with his family, talking briefly to Seth Walters then shooing away the crowd that had gathered, including the two hard-faced men who would have delivered me dead or alive, who went off muttering and shaking their heads.

The captain greeted me warmly. 'This country suits you well,' he told me. 'You have grown tall in the months since I saw you!'

'Jack has helped save my life!' I announced, still clinging tight to my friend's hand. 'He came to find me in the forest and brought me here to claim my pardon!'

The captain smiled down at me. 'You are surrounded by friends who wish you well, Maggie, and I can give you free passage on the *Endeavour* back to England, if you wish it. We set sail in the New Year.'

Once more I had to breathe deeply when I saw that I might return to the old world and my familiar harbour with its fishing boats and boatyards, its old abbey on the hill.

'Do not decide until you are calm and collected,' Captain Andrews advised.

At which his young daughter, Jenny, standing in the flesh before me with the fair hair and bright blue eyes that her father had described to me, set up a clamour with her mother to let me stay with them at their house in Jamestown. 'Maggie must be my playmate. She can have her bed in my room. We will be friends!'

I thought for a moment how it would be to live comfortably and have a fine man such as Captain Andrews watching over me.

But then Grace Walters stepped forward quietly.

215

'Maggie, remember you have a home with us if you wish it.'

And I recalled riding through the sunny fields on horseback and sitting with the baby in the rocking-chair on the porch, singing him softly to sleep.

'Come into the house,' the governor invited, motioning us all out of the cold into a large entrance hall with a log fire roaring in the grate. He saw to it that the others were made comfortable before leading Jack and me into a small room at the side. 'You have much to talk about,' he said before he closed the door.

I went to stand by the window, my hands clasped in front of me, my thoughts spinning.

'What are you thinking?' Jack asked, keeping his distance, not trying to catch my gaze.

'I am thinking of warm, safe nights at home with my father,' I replied. 'The door is locked and the wind is rattling at the window. He is raking through the embers of the fire, snuffing out the candles on the mantel.'

Jack said nothing and let me dream of home.

'I miss him more than I can say.'

'And shall you go back to Whitby with Captain Andrews?' he asked at last.

'Not now,' I replied. 'I have come too far, seen too many things.'

'This is a young country. *You* are young, Maggie.'

I turned to look at Jack.

'Do not say thank you,' he cut in quickly. 'Thank you sounds like a word you say before goodbye.'

I shook my head. 'What shall I do, Jack? Shall I live with Jenny and Mrs Andrews, here in the town?'

'Like a caged bird,' he muttered, then said no more.

In a town with fine houses and churches, warehouses and busy shops, watching the great ships sail across the horizon. In a house with lace at the windows, standing behind a clipped hedge, ignoring the forest and the river beyond.

'Then shall I live with Seth Walters and plant with him in springtime, and dig and hoe the soil? Shall I?'

Jack smiled at this. 'Better,' he said. 'But, Maggie, you could come to Carolina with me. We would sail across Chesapeake Bay and find a warm welcome there. You may plant for my father and dig his soil at my side!'

I opened my eyes wide and looked ahead to a future with honest Matthew and Alice Miller and their sons and daughters. I would awake at sunrise and spend all day in the fields. We would make things grow tall and strong.

But then Jack would be my brother.

'What is the matter?' he asked, seeing my shining eyes cloud over.

'Nothing,' I murmured. Confusion overcame me.

I would live with the Millers and love Jack as a brother. He would call me sister.

'Will you not come to Carolina with me?' he begged.

I let my thoughts whirl and settle. Then I knew how to answer him, plain and simple. To begin with, there was a question – the first of many. 'How many days from Seth's farm is your home?'

'Two days across country on horseback, one day by sea.'

'So I might come and visit whenever I wish?'

He nodded slowly, a shadow of disappointment passing across his bright hazel eyes.

'And should you be glad to see me?'

Another nod. 'Nothing would please me more.'

'And when I am grown tall and strong, so the wind does not knock me over like a feather, might you think of me as more than a child to take care of – I mean, as a woman?'

For a moment he was startled and his face blushed red. 'I do not think of you as a child now, Maggie.'

'Or as a sister?'

'No.'

'Good.' I knew my decision. 'Go back to Carolina, Jack. Work hard. Wait for me.'

'And what shall you do, Maggie?' He came and stood close to me, searching for the answer in my eyes.

'I shall live with Seth and Grace,' I told him, my heart beginning to soar. 'I shall be happy there, and at quiet times I shall walk in the forest, and who knows, I may meet old friends there.'

Jack smiled and nodded. 'I shall be in Carolina, helping my father. The sun will beat down on our fields and I will know that the same sun beats down on you.'

'I will look up at the stars and think of you, Jack.'

'And in the end you will come to me?'

Think of it – my dark, benighted life had ended. I had stepped into the sun.

'Believe me,' I murmured. 'There is no ocean so wide nor mountain range so high that could keep me away!'

Jack took my hand. 'Then, Maggie Nightingale, let us go and tell them our news,' he said.